D0567032

The Urbana Free Library

To renew materials call
217-367-4057

St. Patrick's
Bed

By Terence M. Green from Tom Doherty Associates
Shadow of Ashland
Blue Limbo
A Witness to Life
St. Patrick's Bed

Also by Terence M. Green
Children of the Rainbow
Barking Dogs
The Woman Who Is the Midnight Wind

St. Patrick's
Bed

Terence M. Green

A TOM DOHERTY ASSOCIATES BOOK
NEW YORK

ST. PATRICK'S BED

Copyright © 2001 by Terence M. Green

Excerpts from *Memories, Dreams, Reflections* by C. G. Jung, copyright 1963, are reprinted by permission of Random House, Inc.

This book is printed on acid-free paper.

Design by Angela G. L. Arapovic

Map by Mark Stein

A Forge Book
Published by Tom Doherty Associates, LLC
175 Fifth Avenue
New York, NY 10010

www.tor.com

Forge® is a registered trademark of Tom Doherty Associates, LLC.

Library of Congress Cataloging-in-Publication Data
Green, Terence M.
    St. Patrick's bed / Terence M. Green.
      p.   cm.
    "A Tom Doherty Associates book."
    ISBN 0-765-30043-5
    1. Stepfamilies—Fiction.   2. Birth fathers—Fiction.   3. Ashland (Ky.)—
Fiction.   4. Ireland—Fiction.   I. Title: Saint Patrick's bed.   II. Title.

PR9199.3.G7574 S7   2001
813'.54—dc21

                                           2001033975

First Edition: September 2001

Printed in the United States of America

0 9 8 7 6 5 4 3 2 1

For Daniel Casci Green,
the completion of my fabulous Trilogy

Acknowledgments

IF YOU'RE lucky, people surround you when you're writing a book, even when they don't know they're surrounding you. Their goodwill, suggestions, patience, advice, anticipation, and outright help all nourish, in ways sometimes too mysterious to articulate. So I have been lucky.

This novel was written with the support of the City of Toronto through the Toronto Arts Council. For their faith and approval and welcome assistance, I am indeed grateful.

My cousins, Jacqueline McCarthy, Jo-Anne and Bob Reid of Madoc, Ontario, did more than their share with warmth and enthusiasm. Rick Conley of Ashland, Kentucky, generously provided me with valuable local information. Gayla Collins of Sheridan, Wyoming, helped me appreciate anew the mysteries of Ashland. In Dayton, Ohio, Dr. Bill Erwin and his wife, Patty, offered a hospitality and largesse second to none, making their city and environs come alive for me. To them I owe a special debt of gratitude.

I want to thank Jim (J. Madison) Davis and his wife, Melissa, Phyllis Gotlieb, Andrew Weiner, Rob Sawyer, Ken and Judy Luginbühl, Ian Lancashire, Tom Potter, Chester Kamski, and Bill and Judy Kaschuk; the good people at

H. B. Fenn: Harold Fenn and his wife, Sylvia, Rob Howard, Melissa Cameron, Heidi Winter, and Kari Atwell; and the terrific folks at Forge Books: Tom Doherty, Linda Quinton, Jennifer Marcus, Jim Minz, and Moshe Feder.

Once again, sincere thanks to my agent, Shawna McCarthy, and double thanks to my insightful editor, David Hartwell.

As always, my sons, Conor and Owen, and my wife, Merle, all surround me with love and support in ways both wonderful and mysterious, letting the writing integrate smoothly into the rich fabric of family.

And then there's Daniel, our new arrival, the ultimate blessing for the new millennium. You don't know how long we've been waiting for you. You helped too. More than you can know.

Talk about luck.

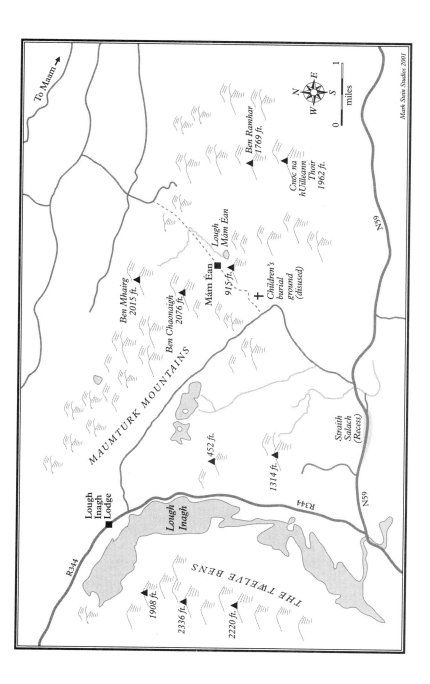

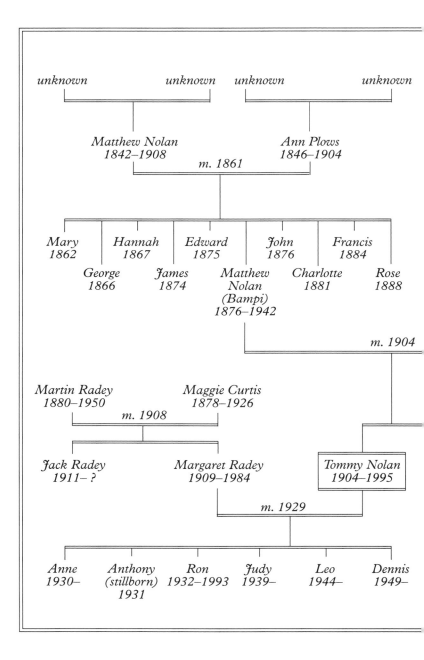

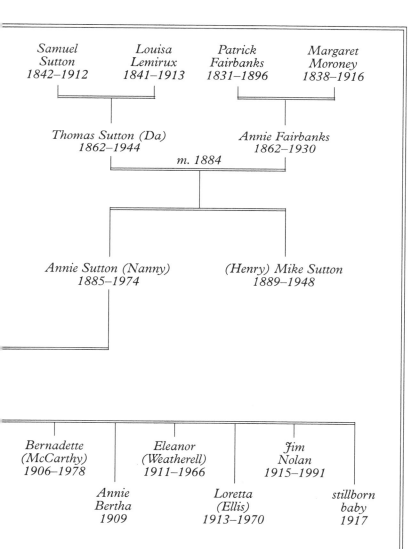

I

Dayton, Ohio

It is important to have a secret, a premonition of things unknown. . . . A man who has never experienced that has missed something important. He must sense that he lives in a world which in some respects is mysterious; that things happen and can be experienced which remain inexplicable; that not everything which happens can be anticipated. The unexpected and the incredible belong in this world. Only then is life whole.

—CARL JUNG
Memories, Dreams, Reflections

One

I

PEOPLE KEEP dying. You'd think I'd be a pessimist, or depressed, or something, but I'm not. I love life. I love being alive. It keeps getting better all the time.

Even though people keep dying.

MY FATHER died on April 15, 1995. He was ninety years old. It was his second bout with pneumonia in six months, and this one did him in.

Up until October of '94 he'd done okay. Almost ninety and never had surgery. Two strokes though. The first was back in 1969, just before his sixty-fifth birthday—just shy of retirement. My mother had said that he worried and fretted about money and retirement so much that he'd given himself a stroke, but he recovered pretty nicely. The second was in 1992, age eighty-seven, which took a lot of the remaining wind out of his sails.

Someone dies at age ninety, after a pretty good life, you don't know whether to cry or say Thank God. I did both.

HE WAS in Toronto General. The hospital phoned me about eleven o'clock at night, then I phoned my brother and sisters, but because I live closest, I was the first one there.

—◇◇◇—

"DON'T TAKE anything out of the room," the nurse said. "Everything has to be accounted for."

I looked at her. "He hasn't got anything."

She put her hands in her pockets, glanced down, left.

But I did slip the red garnet off his finger and put it on my own right hand. It's ten-karat gold, soft and beaten, not worth anything. The stone is squashed down in the setting, lopsided at one end. Later, when he got there, I told my brother, Dennis, what I'd done, wanting his permission, and he understood.

When the nurse came back into the room, she opened the drawer in the bedside table. Inside were his glasses, dentures, and electric razor. That goddamned razor. He loved it. Those last years when he lived with us, he seemed to spend half the time with it spread out in pieces on his night table, screwdriver in hand, glasses pushed up on his forehead, servicing its idiosyncrasies. Then he'd run it around his face and neck long after there was any chance of a whisker hanging on, caressing himself.

His mouth was open, eyes shut. "I'd like the dentures put back in," I said.

She nodded.

And there he was. There it was. The end. Just like that. I couldn't believe it. The rocks and sands of my life had shifted beneath my feet.

I looked down at him. Where are you? I thought. I don't understand. What happened?

I put his glasses and razor in my pocket. I never knew what to do with them, so I still have them.

—◇◇◇—

WE PUT nearly all his clothes in green garbage bags and gave them to Goodwill. Kept his neckties, though. They were kind of interesting. He had a penchant for wine-colored and navy-blue, with white polka dots. One said "Pure Silk, Foulard, Imported by Forsyth" on the label. They were a little wider than the ones that I wore. But you never know. I might wear them. I might.

I still have his tackle box too. I don't know what to do with it either. It's steel gray, covered with rust spots. There's a yellow sticker on the front, just above the latch, that says "Truline—Seamless—Eaton's of Canada." When you lift the lid it unfolds into three trays, and an odor steals out that takes me back to childhood in a wooden rowboat, then disappears.

Inside is my father.

The hula popper, with the rubber grass skirt rotted away. Then the rest of the names crystallize: flatfish, crazy crawler, jitterbug, Mepps spinners. There's a trailer chain for keeping fish in the water after a catch, boxes of hooks, razor blades, a hundred yards of eight-pound test line, leaders, sinkers, a pair of pliers, a Langley Fisherman's De-Liar scale. And then there's the wooden, handmade hand-painted lure, about four inches long, that we never saw him use. We'd ask him about it, my brother and I. He'd only smile and tell us that it was for muskie. He never fished for muskie.

This is my legacy.

II

LIFE KEEPS surprising me.

I didn't see it coming. I hardly see anything coming.

That night of my father's funeral, when Adam asked about his own father, I was floored. A bolt out of the blue. He'd never asked before. Never mentioned him. Nothing.

In hindsight, I don't know why I was so surprised. Now that I think of it, if he was ever going to ask about his father, that would have been the logical time. But I didn't think of it then.

Hindsight. Like they say. Twenty-twenty.

HE ASKED it simply. "Is my father alive?"

Jeanne and I both stopped chewing.

Adam waited. He's twenty-one now, majoring in English at the University of Toronto, going into third year. He is my stepson. He was ten years old when I met him that summer in Ashland, Kentucky, twelve when we settled here in Toronto, fourteen when Jeanne and I finally married, and I'd always thought that I was the only father in his head.

Like I said, it blindsided me.

And Jeanne. His mother was so taken aback she was speechless for a good thirty seconds.

I watched her, then Adam, waited.

Finally, she nodded. "I think he is. I don't know for sure, but I think he is." Her eyes darted to me, then settled on Adam. They stared at each other in silence.

Then Adam began eating again, patient, calm. We followed his lead. After a minute or so, though, he asked his next question: "Where is he?"

I looked again at Jeanne, then Adam. When she caught my eye I said, "Why don't I get us all some coffee?"

ADAM IS a big, good-looking kid. I still thought of him as a kid, even though I was staring at his dark five o'clock shadow and his hands on the table in front of him were bigger than mine. But twenty-one. When you're fifty-one like I am, twenty-one is hardly on the map.

Looking at him, though, digesting his question, unsettled by my own new loss, a collage of myself at his age drifted back: the 1960 Chev Impala with 111,000 miles on it, my job as a truck driver's helper, delivering office furniture around the city, the summer of '64, the Beatles. Girls. Drinking. Living in my parents' basement. Girls.

Adam was a quiet kid. You start being quiet around your parents at puberty. Too much stuff going on inside. But sliding free from my flash of nostalgia, watching his patience after dropping his bombshell, I realized that he was definitely on the map, and had been for a long time.

ADAM NEVER called me Dad. It was always Leo. When he was twelve, shortly after we'd moved here, he asked me why there were cracks in the wall and ceiling of his room.

"I haven't painted them yet," I said.

"I don't mean that. I mean how do the cracks get there in the first place. If a house is built properly, shouldn't there be no cracks at all?"

I shrugged. "The house is old."

He was quiet, considering it.

"Must be sixty years old," I continued. "Houses settle. Cold and heat, expansion, contraction. It just happens."

He was sitting in his bed. I remember that it was winter, that it was cool, that his room needed better storm windows.

He waited for more. But I didn't tell him anything more. I didn't tell him that everything settled, everything cracked, that the rocks and sands shifted beneath your feet. I knew that he would find out for himself soon enough.

MY FATHER always made instant coffee, but we've got a new Philips Café Classic. I paid about sixty bucks for it at Zeller's, and within a month, somewhere in its innards a hose clamp came loose, flooding the kitchen counter with hot water. I ignored the warning on the bottom cover ("Do not remove—repair should be done by authorized service personnel only"), unscrewed it, and fixed it with needle-nosed pliers. Its parts spread open, exposed, it was, I realized at the time, a lot like an electric razor.

That night, I poured three cups from it, black, set them on the kitchen table.

"HOW COME you never asked before?" Jeanne sipped the coffee, watching her son.

Adam hesitated, seemed to think about it. But I guessed that he'd already thought about it a lot. "Didn't seem to be important."

"Why is it important now?"

He shrugged.

"Is it because of Gramp?"

Gramp was my father. Tommy Nolan.

"Maybe."

"It's only natural."

"Were you ever going to tell me?" he asked suddenly.

I sat still, watching them, seeing new things, things I hadn't seen before.

"I told myself I'd tell you whatever you wanted to know if you ever asked. Well"—she tucked the loose strand of hair behind her ear, like she always did—"you've asked."

I cradled my cup in both hands, feeling its warmth. Waited.

"HE WAS in Dayton, last I heard. Dayton, Ohio. But that was a long time ago. Maybe he's not there anymore. I don't know." Jeanne paused, did some more thinking. "You're twenty-one, Adam. He left before you were born. That's a long time. I haven't seen him since." She fixed her eyes on him. "I've always believed that it wouldn't serve you well to speak ill of him, so I never spoke of him at all." She sighed. "The long and the short of it is that he knew I was pregnant and he left. He didn't want to get married. Your Aunt Amanda met him on the street in Cincinnati, must've been fifteen years ago. It was him spoke to her. She told me how she couldn't believe his nerve, coming up to her like that."

I listened to the Kentucky drawl that she had never lost, that I would never want her to lose.

"He told her he was working in a factory in Dayton. That's how I know what I know."

"Did Aunt Amanda tell him about me?"

"She told me she said to him that he had a son, and that he should go see him, do something about it, do what was right. But I never heard from him. He never called, nothing. This was about five years before Leo and I met. Leo's your daddy, honey. He's the one helped me raise you. He's the one helped put food on the table, pays for your schooling. You know that."

"I know it." He looked at me. "You've been great, Leo. You know I know that." He shook his head. "But this isn't anything against Leo. And it's not meant to upset you, Mom." He folded his left hand into a fist and held it against his chin, under his lower lip. "I don't know," he said. "I don't know."

None of us knew. This was a new place. We hadn't been here before.

III

THAT NIGHT was the night of the first dream.

I dreamed I heard footsteps coming up the stairs, thought it must be Adam. When I saw him, though, it was my father, wrapped in old, frayed towels mottled with bloodstains. I remember remarking that it was a disgrace the way those with whom he was staying were taking care of him.

When I woke up, it took me a long time to get back to sleep.

IN THE morning, dressing, I reached for my watch and rings—part of the daily ritual. I keep them on the book-shelf by my bed in a four-by-six ashtray that Jeanne bought me for $1.29 in Las Vegas. And I don't even smoke. Nobody in our house smokes.

It's adorned with a back-shot of three girls in thong bikinis, legs dangling in a pool. Adam tells me those bikinis are called butt-floss. You can always learn stuff from kids.

My watch, my wedding ring, and my father's ring.

Only the red garnet—my father's ring—wasn't there.

Puzzled, I looked on the floor, on the shelf behind the tray, even on my finger. I saw it in the center of the dresser.

I had no memory of leaving it there. In fact, I had a distinct memory of studying it, then placing it in the ash-tray, a new nightly addition.

I rubbed my forehead.

When I opened the drawer with my socks and underwear, his glasses and razor were sitting there staring at me. I was sure that I had left them on the night table in his old room down the hall.

Sliding the garnet on the ring finger of my right hand and the wedding band on the same finger of my left, I strapped on the watch, took out clean socks and underwear, and closed the drawer.

I turned and watched Jeanne sleeping, auburn hair tousled, to me, beautiful. I thought of Adam, equally beautiful, sleeping in his own room—its walls lined with new cracks, fissures that would keep opening no matter how many coats of paint were rolled over them—thought how lucky I was to have my whole family with me even while I slept.

And I looked at my hand. Looked at the ring.

Saw him on the stairs, in the night, coming up to get me.

LATER THAT day, I put his tackle box in the basement, behind the furnace.

Two

I

FOR A man like me, to have a woman is to have a destiny. Before I met Jeanne, I was going nowhere, heading for middle age like everybody's uncle, off to work daily, making meals for myself, staying comfortable, living in a one-bedroom apartment here in Toronto. Taking no risks. Jeanne changed everything.

We met back in 1984, after my mother died, when I traveled down to Ashland, Kentucky, on that family thing. Looking for my mother's brother, Jack. It's a long story, one that I'll save for another time.

We needed each other. Adam and I too. It was good. It still is. In fact, it's better than good. I've got a destiny now.

I'D NEVER met anyone like Jeanne. Hell, I'd never even been to Kentucky before. She was waitressing in Woolworth's, but gave it all up, that fabulous career and all its myriad opportunities, to follow me, a northerner, here to Toronto, to another country.

She had told me about Adam and his father's epic indifference on our first real date, that night in Ashland at the Chimney Corner Tea Room, on Carter near Fifteenth. It had baffled me then, and it baffles me now even more.

Since then I've heard lots more stories. I heard how strict her father was, how he wouldn't let her talk on the phone on a school night when she was a teenager, how he'd unscrew the phone's mouthpiece and keep it with him when he went upstairs to bed or out for the evening. And I got one of my first indicators of just how resourceful she could be when she told me that she went down to a phone booth on Winchester and unscrewed the mouthpiece from the phone there and kept it in her purse as a spare. There was no stopping her.

And when she'd gotten pregnant, I heard how she and her mother collaborated on the story that she was going to work in Cincinnati—live with her sister, Amanda, and her husband—to keep the truth from her father. His discipline and strictness were the stuff of family legend. ("Mark my words" was the catchphrase that reverberated throughout that little house.)

She had Adam in Cincinnati, but she didn't want to live there. She wanted to go home, to Ashland, so she put Adam in a laundry basket, got on the bus, and slipped back to the family home on Carter, east of Thirtieth. I heard about the hand-wringing, the pacing all that afternoon, waiting for her father to come home from work, trying to construct a story, any story, that would help allay his certain outrage and the ensuing volley of condemnation—not to mention his embarrassment and the humiliation at having been the butt of such subterfuge from his own wife and daughter.

Phil Berney had ruled the roost in a pretty old-fashioned way.

And so it happened like this.

"Jeanne's got something she wants to show you, Phil."

These were her mother's words, so the story went.

He was sitting in the big blue easy chair in the living room—the one that's still there—watching the six o'clock news.

Jeanne brought the laundry basket out of the bedroom and set it on the carpet at his feet.

"This is your grandson."

Nobody spoke.

"His name's Adam."

Phil Berney looked at the baby, at his daughter, his wife.

Claire Berney put her hands over her mouth. Without sound, she began to cry.

Jeanne looked at her father. "I'm sorry, Dad. I should've told you."

He still said nothing.

"I was afraid." She looked at her mother. "We were afraid. Of what you'd do, of what you'd say. I thought I was going to give him up for adoption, but I've changed my mind."

She held her ground. Standing in front of him. The baby at his feet.

The silence was a chasm. He was searching for the pieces, trying to understand. Nobody could tell what he was feeling, what he was thinking. And when he spoke, finally, softly, there was no explosion, no anger. "He can't sleep in a laundry basket," he said. He looked at his wife. "He needs a proper crib."

"Dad was nearly always right," Jeanne told me years later. "I can see it now."

The next day Phil Berney went out and bought a crib, and spent the hour after dinner assembling it. It had baseball players painted on the headboard, a ball and glove on the footboard. They think that's why Adam loves baseball so much.

I only knew Phil Berney during that first year I was seeing Jeanne. He died the next summer, when Adam was eleven.

People were still marking his words, even when I knew him.

II

JEANNE AND I were married Friday, September 2, 1988, at the Graceland Wedding Chapel in Las Vegas. It was the Friday before Labor Day, before Adam had to start back to school. He was fourteen. He was my best man.

We'd been talking about getting married for over a year, but couldn't figure out exactly how to do it. Neither Jeanne nor I attended any church regularly—still don't—so that was a problem. There was which city to do it in—Ashland or Toronto. And then there was the cost—the paraphernalia, the attendants, the hall, the reception, the debates about the guest list, the gown, the tux. It went on and on. We got a migraine whenever we talked about it, so it became a topic we didn't know how to deal with.

But there was the fact that we'd been living together, both in Ashland and whenever she and Adam came to Toronto, and the fact was that we were both becoming more conscious of Adam in the middle of our cohabiting. He was a teenager. He knew what was going on. Maybe he had always known, but at age ten or eleven he still seemed to think of Leo only as Mommy's Friend. At thirteen and fourteen, he knew I was more than a friend. What kind of example were we setting? We weren't sure. New territory for both of us. And what the hell. We couldn't stay away from each other. Couldn't keep our hands off each other. Why not get married?

But how to do it.

City Hall was a possibility. It seemed more and more like the logical thing to do. But there was something about being so logical, so conventional, that we stalled, eddied, procrastinated.

It all changed one evening in July of '88.

"READ THIS," I'd said, sliding the newspaper across the kitchen table to Jeanne.

"What is it?"

"Read it."

It was in the Sunday *Toronto Sun*, one of those features that you only find in weekend papers. Not news. Human-interest stuff. The headline was "Goin' to the Chapel." It was datelined Las Vegas.

Jeanne read it quietly. A Toronto couple who had lived together for seventeen years had won a trip to Vegas. Something in the Nevada air, in the cascade of blue and orange neon, had made them decide, after all that time, to tie the knot.

I watched Jeanne's face. She frowned, smiled, frowned again.

"Jesus," she said.

"What?"

"Says there were over eighty thousand weddings there last year. There are forty-two chapels. They take up thirteen pages in the Vegas yellow pages."

I waited a minute. Then I said, "What do you think?"

She looked up, met my eyes, thinking. That bit of smile came back.

THE NEXT day, after work, I went to the Metro Reference Library near Bloor and Yonge and photocopied thirteen pages from the Las Vegas yellow pages.

"YOUR MOTHER and I are thinking of getting married in Las Vegas. What do you think?"

Everything was riding on Adam's reaction. If he turned thumbs down, it was off. Our life was good. We didn't need marriage. At least, we didn't think so.

It was dinnertime. Simple routines had emerged: decisions and food just seemed to go together.

He didn't keep us waiting.

"I think it's cool," he said. Then he added, "My friends will think it's cool."

"Will you be my best man?"

"Sure." He smiled now, pleased.

Jeanne relaxed visibly. You could see it in her face, her shoulders. Her eyes came alive.

That night, at the kitchen table, with Adam and I listening, Jeanne called a handful of the chapels in the photocopied pages that I had brought home. They had 1-800 numbers to make it almost painless. Silver Bell ("Don Johnson, Diana Ross"), Little Chapel of the Flowers ("Elegant Reception Center"), Candlelight ("California Checks Welcomed"), Little White Chapel ("50 Years in the Business of Love!"). There were drive-in weddings, weddings in a plane flying over the Grand Canyon, weddings in a hot tub inside a limousine.

We were more sensible than all that. We selected

Graceland ("Home of the 'King'!"). It was the lady on the other end of the phone who swayed us. No pressure, easy-going, honest, funny. Jeanne asked all the questions, and liked her. We booked it.

We opened a dusty bottle of cabernet sauvignon, poured two glasses, even offered a glass to Adam. He made a face, got a can of Coke from the fridge instead.

When I told my father, later, that we were going to get married in Vegas, that there were eighty thousand weddings a year performed there, he said, "Yeah. And how many divorces."

My father.

JEANNE'S TASTE in music contained a curious twist on Kentucky rockabilly. She had once told me that she preferred music by singers who had died violently in a motorized vehicle. I had to admit, there were plenty of them.

Elvis didn't quite qualify. But he was close. He was close.

For a hundred bucks you got Elvis to sing at your wedding. We splurged. Why not the King? Why not.

JEANNE BOUGHT herself a little white dress. Her mother, Claire, was her maid of honor. The four of us went: me, Adam, Jeanne, and Mrs. Berney. We picked the Hacienda Hotel. I sprang for a room for her mom, one for Adam, one for us. Claire Berney had never stayed in a hotel in her life. She thought she had died and gone to heaven.

Graceland did a good job. Seriously. Elvis was great. I remember that the minister's first name was Rudy, and that he was sensitive and kind about the whole thing. Cost, including Elvis, the limo ride to and from the hotel, flowers, video—the works—was three hundred and some dollars. Of course, that's not counting the air fares, which backed up my Visa card for a couple of years afterward.

Jeanne keeps a five-dollar casino chip from the Hacienda Hotel in her purse as a memento. My hair was thin even then. I bought a hat at a shop in the Hacienda, to protect my head from the Nevada sun—an ivy cap that I wore till it fell apart. The one I wear now is a replacement.

A couple of years later, back home, on the six o'clock news, I watched them detonate the Hacienda, watched it collapse in a cloud of dust, onlookers roped back at a safe distance.

Three

I

WHEN I was twenty-two or twenty-three, my Uncle Jim, Dad's younger brother, took me to a Legion Hall that he frequented for a couple of beers and a game of pool. I liked Jim. He drove my father crazy.

In his youth, Jim had gotten into trouble with the law and with his parents and with my father and mother. There were streams of stories. We'd heard how, in the thirties, he and a group of teens from Northern Vocational stole a car to drive to a dance at Lake Wilcox north of Toronto, how they drank, argued about who would drive home, how the keys got thrown into the bush. The details of his arrest are blurry, but he ended up in the Don Jail. The end of the story has Nanny, his mother, making him turkey sandwiches, and Da, her father, his grandfather, getting sent home with the sandwiches after trying to deliver them.

"He's in jail. What're you, crazy?" The man at the front desk hadn't blinked.

When he was caught skipping school, Nanny threw him out and Da threw him back in. Nanny bought him a violin. He sold it. When my mother married my father she went to live in the Nolan family home on Maxwell Avenue. Jim was still there. The pram that my mother had bought for my sister Anne went missing. It came out later: Jim had sold it.

One of Jim's legs was shorter than the other. He had operations on his hip, grafting bone from there to his leg. I heard how when he was a kid, the other kids playing outside, he had to lie on a flat board in the kitchen.

Jim. My father would shake his head. "I used to park my car down at the docks at night," he'd say, "get on the cruise boats, play in the band all night, come back, and be puzzled why I had so little gas left in the tank. One night I came back a little early, the car was gone. I phoned the police. We're standing there filling out the report, up drives Jim. He'd had a key made, took the car most nights."

Jim, he'd say. And shake his head.

"WE WERE all surprised when he married your mother." Jim leaned against the pool table, taking the pressure off his bad leg.

I chalked my cue, looked at him. My uncle. My godfather. Usually he made me laugh, always had a funny story.

"He'd been going with another girl. We all thought he was going to marry her. Then he turned around and married your mother."

It was information that confused me. I wasn't sure I wanted to know.

"He used to go out with a girl down at Port Dover, where he played in the bands in the summer. That was the girl. You ever hear about this?"

"No." I missed my shot, stood back.

"He was quite a ladies' man. I always thought maybe he had other women even after he married your mother. What do you think?"

"I don't know." It was all I could think of to say. Such a thing had never occurred to me. My father was a mystery. All fathers are mysteries.

I NEVER knew what to make of Jim after that. I had trouble understanding why he had told me that story. True or not, there was nothing I could do about it. But why would he tell me such a thing? He was talking about my father.

I've thought about it a lot, and I have an idea now. It's taken me years. I had to get older, have my own set of unfathomable experiences, have life boot me around a bit.

I'd heard another story about Jim, this one from my mother. I'd heard how he and his wife tried and were unable to have children, how when my mother brought me home from the hospital after I was born, he had held me in his arms and said to my mother, "He's beautiful. Can I have him?" No, he couldn't have me. But he could be my godfather.

Jim and Anna Mae had eventually adopted two beautiful boys of their own, raised them strong, fine. Jim remained the likable con man. But he knew how to be a father.

In 1991, when we knew Jim was dying, I took Dad to the hospital to see him. Jim was delirious, had a respirator over his nose and mouth, lungs full of pneumonia. But when I held his hand, he focused, startling blue eyes, stared at me, knew who I was, squeezed hard, and I squeezed back. Hard as I could. He still wanted me. Wanted to be my father. That's why he'd told me the story.

On the way home, in the car, Dad began talking. "Poor Jim," he said. "He had to wear one of those built-up shoes when he was a kid. He hated it. He used to sit on the curb, take it off, and throw it across the street.

"Jim." My father shook his head. I glanced sideways at him. His cheeks were wet.

"Those shoes were expensive," he said.

Heading south back into the city, I could still feel the hand. Squeezing. Hard.

II

TOMMY NOLAN, my father, married Margaret Radey, my mother, on November 30, 1929, and they lived in his family home—the semidetached house at 55 Maxwell Avenue in North Toronto—until she died in 1984. Dad lasted there one more year without her, selling it in 1985.

I grew up in that home. It was crazy. But I now understand that I didn't see the wildest years. They were before my time. Dad was one of five. Three of them as well were still there—Jim, Eleanor, and Loretta—along with his father (Bampi), mother (Nanny), and her father—Dad's grandfather—Da. My sister Anne was born in 1930, my brother Ron in 1932. Eleanor married and left in '32. But Loretta didn't marry until '36, and Jim was there until the early forties—he and Anna Mae weren't married until 1943. My sister Judy came along in 1939. And I forgot to mention my cousin Jacquie, who was born in 1928 and spent most of her youth at Maxwell Avenue, raised by Nanny and my mother, after Jacquie's mother's marriage fell apart (her mother was Berna, my father's sister, who married in 1926, before my father did).

My parents had nine children, but only five of us survived. There were a couple of stillbirths and twins that died at birth. Mom only named one of them—Anthony, in 1931. He was her second baby, the first boy, and she carried him around in a secret place inside herself as long as I knew her. There was even a statue of St. Anthony on a dressing table in her bedroom, which I used to study as a child. When you lose something, you pray to St. Anthony, she told me. He's the patron saint of lost things. Then the story would come out. St. Anthony, I came to understand, stood for the other babies too—and for everything else my mother had lost.

Nineteen thirty to 1949. She had babies for nineteen years, from age twenty to thirty-nine. By the time my brother Dennis and I appeared in the mid- and late forties, the place had virtually cleared out. In comparison to the thirties, the house must have seemed either like a ghost town or like paradise. Nanny, my father's mother, was still there though, a fixture as I grew up, sitting in the green, cloth-covered chair in the living room, watching *The Edge of Night* every afternoon on the RCA black-and-white TV. She didn't die until 1974, age eighty-nine.

The house had three bedrooms. The basement was full too. The place was crazy.

LIKE I said, when Mom died, Dad lasted a year in the house alone. Then he sold it, moved to a senior citizens' apartment on Yonge Street. He was there for three years—1985 to '88.

In the spring of '88, I went to see him and made a pitch.

"JEANNE AND I are going to buy a house together. Here, in Toronto."

Dad now occupied the green, cloth-covered chair, only now it was in his apartment at Fellowship Towers. The arms were more frayed than ever. He was watching TV. He always watched TV.

"Oh? You getting married?"

I was married a long time ago. It ended after three years. My one and only try. Fran. I shrugged. "Not yet. We've talked about it. Probably. But right now, we just want to do this."

"Mm." He pondered. "Adam?"

"He'll start high school here."

He looked at me. "It's a big step."

"I know."

"Living together."

I nodded.

"Don't see what's wrong with people just living together. Couldn't do it in my day." Then he thought about it. "Well, you could do it. But it wasn't easy. Most people looked down on you, like you were doing something really wrong."

"Like Berna." I mentioned his sister. She had died in '78.

"Like Berna. Ma nearly had a fit." He shrugged. "Doesn't matter now, does it?"

"No, it doesn't."

"Where you going to buy? Got a place picked out?"

"That's what I wanted to talk to you about."

He waited. Even though he was looking at me, I knew he wasn't seeing much of me, just like he wasn't seeing much of the TV. His eyes were going. Macular degeneration. Still, he managed to get around. Good instincts, I thought. Good sense. Radar.

"You could come to live with us."

He paused, surprised. Then: "Nah. Wouldn't work. Besides, I like it here. It's a good spot."

"I know that. The thing is, though, we could do each other a favor."

He sat back.

"Jeanne and I can buy a place of our own. That would be fine. But if you come to live with us, we'd buy a bigger place so that you could have your own quarters, as separate as possible. You just pay us the same rent as you're paying here. Your finances stay the same. Hell, they'll be better. It'll include food too. Room and board."

He was quiet, thinking.

"Meals . . . We'll work it out. We'll work everything out. It'll be a work-in-progress."

A long silence.

"What do you think?" I waited.

"What's Jeanne think of it?"

"She likes the idea."

"Really?"

"Really."

More silence. Then: "And Adam?"

"Adam likes you. You like Adam."

He nodded. "Mm. I don't think these things usually work out. Your mother didn't like living with Nanny." He had a small reverie. "I made a mistake not getting our own place as soon as we were married." A pause. "Suppose it doesn't work out. Suppose we get on each other's nerves. What then?"

"Good question. I don't know what to say. There are no guarantees for anything, this included. Let's just say that it's not a one-way street." I looked at him sitting there, my father, in his eighties. "If it doesn't work out, you can come back here. Things can be reversed. Not without a few scrapes, but certainly without any major damage. We wouldn't let anything get that far."

He was still thinking. Then aloud: "I'm not going to get any better, you know. I'm only going to get worse."

I ignored him. "Adam could use a grandfather. You'd have a role. There'd be somebody in the house when we were out. I'd like that."

He pressed the mute button on the TV, stared at the silent images. "You know," he said, "fellow in the next room died last week. I've got a spare key. I found him. He was sitting in a chair just like this." He gripped the worn arms. "Shook me up. Made me realize that some stranger was going to come in one day and find me sitting here, just like him."

I waited a minute before trying again.

"If you don't want to do it, I understand. But we'll buy a smaller house—we'll have to—and it'll be too late. Now's the time. We'd buy a house to suit." A pause. "You'd be living in sin with us. At your age. Think about it." I smiled.

He stared at the television's silent, flickering images.

"You could eat Mexican food with us."

He turned, looked at me, still silent.

JEANNE AND I bought a big, old semidetached house in the South Riverdale section of the city. My brother Dennis and I moved Dad's belongings in the day after Jeanne and I and Adam had moved our own stuff in.

He had this old table lamp, white shade, milky glass base shaped like a cluster of grapes. It was his mother's—

Nanny's. It had been at Maxwell Avenue—one of the things he had kept. Dennis and I dropped it, chipped the base. There's a rough edge now, a hunk an inch or so missing.

The lamp's another thing of his that I still have.

Four

I

ADAM BROUGHT it up again a week or so later. I was watching a ball game on TV in the kitchen as I did the dinner dishes. Jeanne was on the phone upstairs talking with her mother.

He came in, sat down at the kitchen table.

"You going out later?" I rinsed a plate, set it in the dishwasher, picked up another.

"Yeah. Going to meet Jane. Go for a coffee."

I nodded.

"Down in the Beaches. Queen Street."

"Nice evening. Cool, but nice." I squirted dishwashing liquid into an aluminum pot, worked the yellow nylon scrubby against the burned sediment stuck to its bottom.

"I think I'd like to go to Dayton this summer. See my father."

I stopped scrubbing the pot, looked at him.

"You're not upset, are you, Leo?"

I had to think. "No," I said. "A little surprised, though." I straightened. "Told your mother?"

He shook his head. "Not yet."

I dropped the scrubby in the sink, rinsed my hands, tore off a piece of paper towel. "I don't know what to say."

He looked at me.

"Honestly."

"I know."

"Maybe it's a good idea." I dried my hands, dropped the towel in the wastebasket. "I don't know." I waited a few seconds, then: "You might be moving too fast. Maybe it's not a good idea. You don't know anything about him. We don't even know if he's still there." I hesitated. "Does he even want to see you is another very real question, don't you think?"

He toyed with the salt and pepper shakers in front of him. "Did you ever wish you knew more about your father? About Gramp?"

"Yes." I leaned back against the counter. I watched Adam frown, run his fingers along the contours of the shakers. "Lots of times. Especially now."

"That's the way I feel."

"I understand."

"Like I have to know. Have to get it straight in my head."

I let him talk.

"Who he is. What happened. You know."

I nodded. "I know."

"Do you think I'll be disappointed?"

"Depends on what you're looking for."

"I don't know what I'm looking for."

"Most of us don't."

WHEN MY father had moved in with us back in '88, after one night's sleep in his new room, he told us that he'd slept like a baby. And when he woke, he said, there were kids playing outside in the back alley. He said it was a treat to hear, especially after where he'd been, living with so many old folks.

His life at Fellowship Towers was something that I knew little about. Three years there.

There was a lot of him that I didn't know anything about.

BECAUSE NANNY was the oldest, we had to defer to her. My mother told us so. This was what we heard all through my childhood on Maxwell Avenue. You can't have a bath on Thursday nights. That's Nanny's night for a bath. That's Nanny's chair. You get up and let her have it. We're going to watch *Ed Sullivan*. Nanny likes it.

The word "matriarch" was one that I didn't know back then.

My father was mostly quiet.

When his mother—Nanny—died in '74, Dad's brother Jim had a flask of whiskey at the funeral home. He kept disappearing downstairs into the washroom, coming back up smelling of rye, wanting my father to go with him next time. Dad drank pretty stupidly when he wanted. I'd seen it. We'd all seen it. But he wouldn't go with Jim then.

Back at the house, after Nanny was buried, my mother sent me out for a bucket of KFC chicken and served it to the family and guests that had come back with us. There was some more drinking, some coffee, small socializing. Jim was there. Suddenly my father said, "I have to go upstairs." I can still hear his voice. It was raspy. Soft. Like something was caught in his throat. No tears, though. "I have to lie down." I watched him climb the stairs. He went into his bedroom, the sanctuary he and my mother had from his mother, from us, closed the door. He stayed there until the next morning.

I think of that climb up the stairs every now and then, wonder if my dream of him on the stairs is related.

I have a lot of memories of people, myself included, on those stairs. I'm not sure why.

"I WON'T try going to see him until later in the summer." Adam pushed the salt and pepper shakers away. "Got to make some money first."

"Makes sense."

I looked at him. What I felt was an impossible mixture, a quiet ache. I've felt it before and since. It's a flood, a burst, soft, like my father's voice going up the stairs to lie down, to be alone.

When my own son was stillborn, years ago, back when I was with Fran, it was in another life. That life disappeared. It scarcely seems real. It's gone, like my mother, father, my brother Ron, like the past in general. In the here and now, sitting at the table in front of me, talking to me, man to man, was my real son, my only son, alive, needing me.

II

"HE'S GOING to get hurt," Jeanne said. "That's all there is to it."

"You're probably right."

"Why is he doing this? I don't understand. Why?"

"Because he has to." I shrugged. "It's normal. Normal, healthy curiosity." I turned to face her. We were lying in bed.

Searching for someone missing, from the past, was something that I understood. I'd done it. My mother's brother, Jack. He led me to Ashland, down through the States, onto the Ohio River. In the heat and the glare and the smell of oil and steel, in Ashland, I'd found Jeanne and Adam instead. Or as well. I wasn't sure. "Family is a mystery," I said, "that we have to explore."

Jeanne looked at me.

"We can't help it."

She was quiet.

"Adam can't help it."

ANOTHER EVENING, watching baseball on the tube, I said to him: "You're an English major. There are books all around the place. You've read more than I ever have, probably more than I ever will. I envy you."

"You polish off those thrillers pretty well. Nothing wrong with them. They're good. And you like Steinbeck."

"But the courses you get to take. You're lucky. The Modern Novel. Classics in Translation." A pause. "You're lucky." I hadn't gone to university. Right from high school to work. Jeanne hadn't finished high school. My father had only finished grade school. Mom—she was the bright one, the talented one, the sensitive one: some time at the Ontario College of Art, before getting married and joining the ranks of full-time mothers and homemakers.

"I've got a question for you, Shakespeare," I said.

"Shoot."

"Are there any books about fathers and sons? Any classics? Something I should read?"

He sat, thinking.

"I did read *East of Eden*. Long time ago. I guess it qualifies as pretty good. Don't know if it makes the 'great' list or not," I added. "There's even an Adam in it. He's the father, though."

"You read it? The whole thing?"

"Yup."

"Wow."

"Haven't you?"

"Saw the movie. James Dean."

"Teenagers," I said.

"I'm twenty-one."

"He died in a car accident. Your mom liked him."

Adam thought some more.

"Great works that I should know," I said. "You know, like if you want to read the classic about the Depression, you've got to read *The Grapes of Wrath*. Or you want to read the classic about alienated youth, you've got to read *The Catcher in the Rye*. You know. Like that."

"Good question," he said.

I let some time pass. "Well?"

"Very good question. Most of what I can think of is about how fathers and sons fight, or how the relationship is abusive. *Long Day's Journey into Night*. Scary. Newer stuff: Russell Banks wrote a book called *Affliction*. Abusive relationship. Same with Tobias Wolff: *This Boy's Life*. More abuse." Some more thought. "Updike's *Rabbit* books deal with it. They're good. *Death of a Salesman*. Willy and Biff and Hap. Might be as good as it gets." He looked at me. "You're a genius for spotting holes in a fabric, Leo. Next year I'm going to bring it up in one of my seminars—how there's a dearth, a gap." He pondered further. "Maybe if there's no abuse, no fighting, there's no relationship. Nothing worth writing about."

I shook my head. "Ain't so."

Adam looked back at the TV, stared blankly.

"Maybe there's too much. Maybe nobody can get their head around it."

A commercial broke the rhythm of the fourth inning.

"Shakespeare, Hemingway, none of them could handle it. Too big." I looked at him. "I'll get us a beer, right?"

Adam just looked at me. We were both thinking thoughts that couldn't be formed into sentences.

I touched his shoulder as I got up and went into the kitchen.

THAT NIGHT I dreamed of my father as a young man, thirtyish, acting in a play, in something like summer stock. His sleeves were rolled up and his biceps were strong. That's all I can remember.

I have no idea what the dream meant or why I dreamed it. Maybe it had something to do with the discussion of books with Adam. I don't know.

Later, in the dark, when I got up to go to the washroom, a light in the spare room was on. I went in, stood there, puzzled. It was the lamp with the milky glass grapes cluster, with the chipped base. The one Dennis and I had dropped when my father moved in.

I turned it off.

Five

I

WHEN I was a kid—five or six years old—after my father would have a few beers—maybe New Year's, Thanksgiving, something like that, when there were lots of little kids around—he liked to shock us by calling us over and moving his dentures around in his mouth, then taking them out and putting them back in. He'd ask us to take our teeth out and show them to him. Stunned that this could be done, that we'd never known it, we'd all try, puzzled at why we couldn't do it. He always laughed. It was a performance that he staged many times, one he clearly enjoyed giving. I watched him do it years later, to his grandchildren.

Jeanne tells me that she had an aunt who, even though she had an upper plate, also had several bottom teeth missing, and that when she ate peanuts she used her thumb as a bottom tooth.

And I'd heard the story of Dad's sister, Loretta, who once got so drunk that she threw up in the toilet at Maxwell Avenue and accidentally flushed her dentures away.

All of these tales, memories, images flashed through my head, a small cascade of snapshots, when I asked the nurse to put my father's dentures back in, that evening in the hospital, that evening he died.

DENNIS AND I had gone, two dutiful sons, to Morley Bedford Funeral Chapel on Eglinton Avenue to make the necessary arrangements. We'd been there eleven years earlier when our mother died. The place had become a strange touchstone in our lives. The gentleman led us down into the basement to see the display and selection of caskets, arrayed there like new cars in an automotive showroom, complete with price stickers—wood polished and burnished, brass and steel buffed and glinting under the display lighting.

We selected the second cheapest casket of the dozen surrounding us. It was tough ignoring the bottom-of-the-line container, but we raised our sights, ever so slightly, knowing that Dad would not approve of us going any higher. Only a damn fool, he'd say, would spend that kind of money on a coffin. Have to be crazy.

We displayed him and put him in the ground in a #20 H.P. Grey Cloth Casket, manufactured by Bernier, retailing for $895. Even then, though, we didn't get off cheaply. Funeral costs are insidious, and keep on mounting: professional services, transfer cost, shelter for the deceased, full embalming, facilities, automotive, documentation, flowers, cemetery fees, funeral board licensing fee, clergy honorarium, organist, etc.

Cost us nearly five thousand dollars to say good-bye.

I can see Dad shaking his head in disgust, damn fools he'd say, telling us we should have buried him in the backyard.

WHEN I was twenty-one, Adam's age, I once asked my father if he liked his job. He had worked twenty-three years for *The Globe & Mail*, and was finishing up his seventeen-year stint at *The Toronto Star*—two of the city's daily newspapers. He worked in the Circulation Departments.

It's a living, he told me.

At twenty-one, I thought this was sad, but said nothing.

I'm fifty-one now. I work in the Circulation Department of *The Toronto Star*—my twenty-third year. My father got me the job. By the time I was twenty-eight, I was glad to have it, to work steady, to have some security.

I started in 1972. That was the year that my three-year marriage to Fran ended. It was one year after my son was stillborn.

It's a living. But those words mean something different to me now. I'm older.

"I DON'T even know his name," I said.

Jeanne looked at me.

"Adam's father. I don't even know his name."

"Jesus."

Another night, the routines finished, propped up in bed on our pillows, the eleven o'clock news droning on the TV set at the foot of the bed.

She grew silent.

"I didn't mean to upset you."

"The past doesn't go away, does it." It was a statement, not a question.

"No," I said. I thought about it. "It goes somewhere else. It stays, but it moves. Like to another city. You decide if you'll visit or not, if it's worth the trip. Or, sometimes, it comes to visit you, unexpected. Just shows up."

"Bobby," she said.

"Mm?"

"Not Bob, not Robert. Bobby. Bobby Swiss."

I didn't say anything.

"That's his name."

A weather map appeared on the screen at the foot of the bed. The blond woman demonstrated with hand motions the low front that was moving into the area, as if she were smoothing a bedspread.

"The things we do," she said, "the people we think are interesting when we're eighteen." She shrugged, looked down at her hands. "I was a kid."

"EVEN HIS name," she said. "It was exciting." Her foot touched mine beneath the covers. "Not as exciting as Leo Nolan."

"Your foot's cold. That's because you leave them outside the covers at night. I don't know how you stand it. My feet are toasty and warm."

"You're all swaddled up in the blankets all night. You're so warm you sweat in your sleep."

"What does 'swaddled' mean? What kind of word is 'swaddled'?"

She leaned over me, her hair falling forward. "Swaddled is what they do to a mummy when they wrap it up. It's what you do to yourself. You need me to cool you down. You sleep all whacky." She put her other foot on my leg.

I looked at her face.

She tucked her hair behind an ear, smiled.

"You better cool me down." I didn't move. Didn't touch her. The moment might disappear.

She put her head on my shoulder. Finally, I touched her hair.

"I'm okay," I said. "I was eighteen once." I didn't know what more needed to be said. It was the past. Moved away.

To Dayton, Ohio.

RANDY NEWMAN has a song called "Dayton, Ohio, 1903." It's on his 1972 album *Sail Away*. It talks about lazy Sunday afternoons, evokes another, gentler time.

There's another song on the same album called "Last Night I Had a Dream." He sings about how everyone he knows is in that dream. He says he saw a ghost.

I keep seeing a ghost. In dreams too. Like that same night. I'm gambling at the slots in Las Vegas, wearing only a T-shirt and shorts. My father comes up behind me and tells me that I'm a fool. That's the dream. That's all I can remember.

And once again, the red garnet ring wasn't in the Vegas ashtray the next morning. I found it later that day, on the kitchen counter, beside the microwave.

II

LIFE IS about timing. We all know it. Sometimes there seems to be a pattern, sometimes it's all hopelessly random. We meet people at the right or the wrong time in our lives, and based on the timing, we do or we do not have a relationship with them. Timing is everything.

And when the timing is right, you have to gamble. I enjoy a small wager. I like the slots in Vegas. I like the blackjack tables. I like to bet on hockey games, baseball games. My friends tell me I'm a fool, but I don't see it that way. It seems to me that life is a gamble, that every decision we make is a gamble. We're always calculating the odds, at every juncture.

Getting out of bed in the morning is a gamble.

In my dream that night, my father had told me that I was a fool. Maybe he was right. But if he was, it wasn't because I was gambling. It was because we're all fools, some of the time. You can be a fool sitting at home in your room, all alone, not doing anything.

IN THE spring of '85 I helped Dad sell the house on Maxwell Avenue. When it was empty, when everything had been cleared out, I went back for one last look around.

It was strange.

I had grown up there. It was our home before I was born, and after I left it had been the focal point of all extended family activity. We called it Camp Maxwell. Generations of us. Fifty-six years. I knew where the hiding places were in the rafters in the basement, how to put your feet on the hot-air vent under the kitchen table to get warm on winter mornings. I knew which stairs creaked, which doors wouldn't close completely, which windows couldn't be opened no matter how hard you tried.

My mother was sitting in her wheelchair in the kitchen, Nanny sleeping upstairs in her bed, my brother Ron standing by the sink with a beer, laughing, kids running up and down the back stairs to the basement where the madness could boil over.

Empty now. Silent. My footsteps echoing.

When I left, I thought I had closed the door on the past, that I had sealed it up when I had pulled it shut for the last time. But like Jeanne and I said: the past doesn't go away. It just moves somewhere else.

The house on Maxwell moved inside me.

I make a point of driving by it whenever I'm in the vicinity, just to see it. Once I even got out of the car and walked down the driveway, curious what the new owners had done with the backyard.

There's a new front entrance, a new garage, new windows. There's new landscaping—it's got interlocking brick now. And that's only the outside.

I don't want to see the inside. I know what it looks like in there. I just close my eyes. There it is.

DAD TOOK the money from the sale of the house and put it into low-yield GICs—Guaranteed Investment Certificates. I tried to steer him, to advise. He'd listen, then do what he wanted: established, name-brand banks. No trust companies. No risk.

He didn't care. Security and peace of mind were more important than investments that needed managing, more important than high-yield potential. Tommy Nolan was no gambler. He had seen the Depression, been the provider for too long, the elephant on whose back the rest of the family had ridden.

When I lost money in a limited partnership scheme last year, years after he had died, I thought of how he'd tell me that I was a damn fool. Then I heard Phil Berney, Jeanne's father, tell me to mark his words.

As usual, they were both right.

HE WAS meticulous. He kept a brown leather folder in the top drawer of his dresser, which he would show me occasionally. You have to know this, he'd say. You have to know where everything is when I die.

It was almost impossible for me to listen to him when he started up like that. I'd shuck my responsibility, block him out.

I have to trust somebody. I've decided to trust you. You're the executor, he'd say. Everybody's counting on you.

In it he had the original deed to the Mount Hope Cemetery plot, Lot 198, Section 16, dated September 18, 1904, deeded to his grandfather, Matthew Nolan, shoemaker by trade, born in County Cork, Ireland, June 29, 1842. It had been purchased the day after Matthew's wife, Ann, had died. There was a receipt for two dollars for the final Lot Transfer to my father, dated August 20, 1980.

He had baptismal certificates dating back to 1876. There were death certificates for Nanny, his mother, (1974) and my mother (1984).

And he kept a book. It was gray, cloth-covered, an accounting ledger. In it was every family financial transaction he'd ever made: loans and mortgages given to family members, amounts and dates of principal and interest paid. You have to collect these debts, he'd say. It's all in the book if anyone says anything.

He was the elephant. Everybody was riding him.

"WHEN THEY bury me, nobody'll come visit," he'd say.

I heard this lots.

"Worked with a guy," he said once, "who told me he was going to be buried underneath Holt Renfrew on Bloor Street. That way he knew he'd get a visitor. His wife would visit him once a day."

But he was right. Again. I hardly ever go to the cemetery plot. I don't need to. He's like the house: he moved inside of me.

AFTER HE died, I threw away the gray cloth-covered ledger. Never mentioned it to anyone in the family.

I think, deep down, it's what he hoped I'd do. I think he would have approved. Either that, or he'd call me a damn fool.

Six

I

HIS GLASSES. The electric razor. The lamp. His ring. The tackle box. Instant coffee.

OUR OWN lives start long before we're born. Millions of years of genetic encoding funnel down into our great-grandparents, then grandparents, finally parents. I mentioned that Dad had macular degeneration, that his eyes were going. It's something that I worry about myself, since I think I have his eyes, his skin, his hair. Like I have so much else of his. His job even, for God's sakes.

Able to see only shadows, shapes, he'd been certified as legally blind by the CNIB—the Canadian National Institute for the Blind—and given a card with his photo and registration number to carry in his wallet. In his eighties, he liked to ride around the city on the TTC—the public transit system—because he got on for free with his blind pass. He'd visit places and streets he knew from his youth, then come home and tell us how it had all changed. He relished claiming the four thousand dollars or so tax credit available annually as a CNIB registrant—anything, even blindness, to one-up the government. And he told me once with a lilt in his voice that when people came to the door and asked him to sign petitions, whatever, he gladly signed them. I'll sign anything, he'd say. I'm not legally responsible for anything I sign, because I'm blind. And he'd smile the half smile.

You might think, from everything I've told you, that my father's death was the most overwhelming thing that has happened to me. It's not true, not really. My brother Ron's death in '93 derailed me more than I ever imagined it would. He was twelve years older than me, lived in another city. I hardly ever saw him. But his death signaled something powerful in me. Of the five of us, my brothers and sisters and me, he was the first to go. I saw my father's eyes at the service for Ron, weak, disbelieving.

Somebody was going to go first. It was an idea that darted into my head on rare meditative occasions, one I didn't entertain at length. I kept wanting to tell my mother, who died in '84, Do you know what's happened to Ron? It's impossible, I'd say to her. She'd want to know. Somehow, she had to know.

My mother. Good Lord. She was the archetypal mother. Selfless. Naive. If you say you loved your mother, a lot of people tend to squirm, even drop their eyes. It's too sentimental an admission, they feel. It doesn't need to be said. Nuts. It does need to be said. I loved her. In hindsight, I understand how much of my life was spent wanting to please her, to make her happy. One of my favorite memories is of her carrying me along Eglinton Avenue, my head on her shoulder, me half asleep. I was the fourth of five. She didn't have me until her mid-thirties, so I know she was around forty when this happened. I know now how exhausted she must have been. And at age fifty-one, I know how much I'd like to put my head back on her shoulder, have her hold me, comfort me, stroke my hair. Just once.

Mom's death, and the death of my son. Stillborn. We were going to call him Aidan. These were the watershed events. These were the ones that rocked my foundations, changed everything.

Dad's death was different. It didn't have the same sense of incompletion. I'd had a chance to wrap up my relationship with him in a way that I had not with the others. I'm sure it was why I hoped that he would live with us for his final years.

I think of his half smile, of his pleasure at beating the government with a four-thousand-dollar tax credit, of signing forms for which he wanted no responsibility, and I understand that he taught me that happiness was a choice that we make.

II

APRIL. MAY. June.

Adam got a job for the summer in The Book Cellar on the Danforth, perfect for him. I was glad. He'd sworn he couldn't take another summer at Mr. Lube, staring up at the undersides of cars, draining crankcase oil. Jeanne's work in the cafeteria at St. Michael's Hospital carried on, unabated. My job at the *Star* droned on further into the summer.

Bobby Swiss and Dayton, Ohio, hovered, hushed shadows behind our lives, daring us to look at them, ponder them. Waiting to step into the light.

Later in the summer, Adam had said.

We waited. Silent.
Maybe it would all go away.

IT DIDN'T go away. I had another dream.

Some dreams are blurs. If you describe them out loud, or write them down, they exist. Otherwise, they evaporate, morning mist rising, burned off by the sun. Others are as vivid and hard as colored glass. This was one of those.

A PUB in Ireland. I know it is Dublin. I'm drinking Guinness. The street signs visible through the windows are in Irish and English. The man across from me is a young man, in his twenties, regaling a group of us with stories. He is familiar, but I can't place him. Then I see the red garnet ring on his right hand and know that it is my father, and he says, "Without any pressure, there is nothing at stake," but I do not understand.

Suddenly I am outside, in the mist and the rain. There are birds. Starlings, everywhere. The Irish has disappeared from the street signs. It is not Dublin, but an American city. There is a different feel, a texture, the rain is not as soft. And in the pub window, no longer Guinness, Kilkenny, but Budweiser, Miller signs, orange and blue neon. Neon like Vegas. I clutch American dollar bills in my hand.

But I am not in Vegas. I know where I am. I see a sign on a building, carved in stone: "Greyhound Bus Station, Dayton." I am in Dayton, Ohio.

WHEN I awoke, Jeanne was there, wiping the mist and rain from my head, my shoulders. "You're having one of your night sweats. You haven't had them since you were sick."

Since I was sick. A flood of images rose up out of the

darkness, out of the shadows and memories of our trips together and why we took them.

Her hand was cool on my brow.

Even though I was awake, the dream was still there. I was half in, half out, swimming up out of that place where dreams swirl like whirlpools, drawing us down.

And that's most of what I remember.

THEY SAY that the Sumerians, more than five thousand years ago, chiseled their dreams onto clay tablets. And I read once that archaeologists discovered a two-thousand-year-old Egyptian book on dream interpretation.

In the clear light of the morning, I looked up Dayton in my road atlas, traced my finger along I-75, the blue line through Ohio. *Bowling Green, Cygnet, Findlay. Bluffton, Lima, McCartyville. Pigua, Troy, Tipp City.* Beads on a string. Like beads on the rosary I held as a child, seated on a cool wooden pew at the back of St. Monica's Church, my mother and father on either side of me. Each town a prayer, a reflection, a step toward the past that must become the present.

III

DAD NEVER knew what to make of nachos. What is this? he'd say.

Nachos. Corn chips, cheese, green onion, jalapeño peppers. You dip it in the salsa. You want a beer?

What're we having for dinner?

This. This is dinner. We'll have some green pea soup too.

How can this be dinner?

I laughed. It just is.

This is something you eat while you watch a hockey game. If you don't have any popcorn. Or ice cream, he added. But not dinner.

Eat it. You'll enjoy it. It's not like we have it every night. It's a change of pace. A treat. Fun.

Fun, he repeated.

I laughed again.

He ate it. He ate all of it. But he knew it wasn't dinner. The soup came the closest.

WE DEVELOPED routines that worked. Because we had strict time lines, Jeanne and I and Adam would get up in sequence in the morning, use the bathroom, shower, eat whatever breakfast we could force-feed ourselves, then off to work and school. After we had gone, after the house was empty and no one was around to pressure him, Dad would get up and dress and use the bathroom at his own pace, running that crazy electric razor all over his face forever. We'd find various pills on the bathroom floor on a daily basis. He had them for everything. He actually liked taking them. He'd line the little bottles up like soldiers. His devotion to doctors and pills was a religious faith— unshakable.

Then it was downstairs for cereal, juice, coffee. The coffee was from the pot I made every night and timed to start perking at six-thirty in the morning. Even with his bad eyes, there was nothing he couldn't handle in that routine, and he'd leave the dishes in the sink for me. Dishes were my domain. Jeanne would claim at parties that her hands never touched dishwater, and I took foolish pride in my work.

I made him a lunch every night, along with lunches for Adam, Jeanne, and myself. All he had to do was fish it out of the refrigerator when he wanted it. Dinners he ate with us. Jeanne handled them. That was her domain. She liked cooking and she was good at it—said that having a glass of red wine while making dinner was like therapy, as good as yoga.

And he always knew when she was working late or had gone out for the evening. Nachos. Or take-out chicken. It wasn't the same.

But he'd eat whatever you gave him. He was grateful.

I learned that from him too.

"WHAT HAPPENED to your father?" I asked him once. He never spoke of his father. It was always Da he mentioned, his grandfather, Nanny's father.

He was quiet for a minute. Then he said, "He went senile."

I listened.

"I remember one time he came downstairs at two o'clock in the morning. He was carrying a candle and had his feet wrapped up in rags. I had just come in. I asked him what he was doing. He told me he was going to work." He paused. "He hadn't worked in years."

I didn't know him. He died in 1942, before I was born. Even Da outlived him, dying in '44. "What did he used to work at?"

"He was a shipper, then a driver, at Doyle Fish Company, down in the St. Lawrence Market. When he got older, he worked for the city. Department of Streets and Cleaning." He paused. "He had a twin brother that died at birth. It was a big family. He was one of ten."

I waited. He didn't offer any more. "Why was he called Bampi?"

"Your sister Anne started that. When she was little she couldn't say Grampa. It came out Bampi. The name stuck. We all liked it."

"Did he have Alzheimer's?"

He looked at me. "I don't know. I never thought of it."

"It sounds like Alzheimer's."

He was thinking. "I never heard of Alzheimer's until the last few years. Some people just went senile. It was the thirties. Happened in lots of families." He looked distant. "Never thought about it before."

"Sounds like it. It was just a thought."

He didn't say anything more. He was quiet for the rest of the evening.

I LIVED with him for seven years, from when he was eighty-three till he died at age ninety. He never mentioned Bampi again.

IV

AT THE Metro Reference Library I asked for the white pages of the Dayton, Ohio, phone directory. The woman at the Information desk gave me a small envelope of microfiche transparencies, showed me how to use the machine, then left me alone.

There was a "Swiss, B" on the black-and-white screen before me. Only one. I read the address, the phone number, copied them on a piece of paper, put the paper in my shirt pocket.

I sat back.

I saw my father, traveling around the city, blind, revisiting places from the past, coming home and telling me how everything had changed. I touched the piece of paper in my pocket. Another step toward becoming my father.

Seven

I

WHAT ELSE can I tell you about Jeanne? Besides everything, I mean. It sounds corny to keep mentioning how we're crazy about each other, but it's true. Most people don't believe us. Everyone is sure we're not being honest, hiding something—a discordant note that would make our relationship more akin to their own experience.

I don't know. I've had lots of relationships that didn't work—most of them, for God's sake. A failed marriage even. But this one works, and it probably shouldn't. And maybe I shouldn't be so smug. After all, no one gets married thinking it isn't going to work, do they? I didn't that first time. Yet half of them don't make it—and of those that do, I don't know how many of them I'd say were real good.

High maintenance, low maintenance. This is Jeanne's theory.

"Most of the women I know treat their pets better than they do their man," Jeanne told me one day. "They got a dog, they'll get up early to walk it, scoop behind it, clean, feed, groom, ooh and aah, pick fleas off it, you name it. Yet they ignore their man. Like they'd be happier if he was gelded. Like their dog."

"Who are you thinking of?"

"Nearly everybody. They like them to bring home a lot of money, wear knee socks and shorts in the summer and mow the lawn, shovel the snow in the winter, and by and large leave them alone. Only a few exceptions." She thought for a moment. "Jenny and Walt. Jenny understands her man." Pause. "Christine and Fred. They're both happy as clams." Longer pause. Shrug. "That's about it. Jenny and Christine get it. Rest of them don't."

"Get what?"

"Lust makes the world go round." Her eyes twinkled.

I nodded sagely. "You'll get no argument from me."

"Course I won't. It's true."

"What about Ted and Irma?"

"What about them?"

"Aren't they exceptions? They seem pretty happy."

More thought. Then: "Nah. She's a little bit nuts."

"Why?"

"She actually does have a dog. She thinks he needs braces."

I laughed.

"Says he has an overbite. God knows what she thinks about Ted."

"Scratch behind my ears?"

A smile.

"Straighten my tail?"

She crooked her finger, twice, beckoning. "You come over here and I'll rub your belly."

It was my turn to smile.

"Women are high maintenance. Men are low maintenance."

It was true. It was profound. She was a genius.

Her finger called me twice more, like underwater sea grass, undulating.

I think I salivated and panted. In fact, I'm sure I did.

THEN THERE was the time—earlier that summer—that she told me that she was a logistical genius—as well as a sexual one, of course.

"I didn't know you knew the word 'logistical,' " I said.

"I know a lot of words, smart guy."

I nodded. "If I turn off the lights, will you whisper some of them in my ear?"

"That's part of my sexual genius. This is different."

I waited. "You have my full attention."

"Adam's car ran out of gas this morning on his way to work."

Adam had a 1990 Toyota Tercel. It functioned for him much the way my 1960 Chev Impala had for me at his age.

"He had to leave it on Logan, near Gerrard. He phoned and told me about it after he finally got to work—late—said he couldn't get away from the store. Asked me if I'd do him a favor—take my car and get some gas, put it in his car, because he didn't have a gas can and it was too far to carry it even if he did have one."

I was trying hard to follow.

"So I did. Got his spare keys from his room, got a can of gas from the corner. They made me leave a twenty-dollar deposit on the damn thing. Poured the gas into his car, then got to thinking."

I frowned.

She smiled slyly.

"This is where the genius part comes in." I folded my hands.

"Pure genius," she said.

"I'm hanging on your every word."

"So I started thinking," she said, "about how pleased and surprised he'd be if I could get his car to him so that he'd have it right after work. Have it sitting there in the parking lot behind the store."

"The perfect mother."

"And wife."

"And wife. Of course."

"But I had my own car with me."

I listened. Smiled. Patient. No idea where this was going.

"I couldn't drive two cars at the same time."

"Can't see how," I said.

"And I didn't want to leave my own car there."

I sat back then, bemused, crossed my arms.

"So I drove my car for two blocks, got out, locked it, went back to Adam's, drove it two blocks ahead of mine, got out, locked it, walked back to my car, drove it two blocks ahead of Adam's . . ."

"You didn't."

"I did."

I laughed.

She beamed. "Took me half an hour."

"All the way to The Book Cellar."

"That's right. Put it in the lot behind the store. Went in and told Adam. He told everyone in the store that his mother was a logistical genius."

"That's where you heard it."

"From my very own son. One genius begets another."

"I'm the luckiest guy in town. Surrounded by geniuses."

I raised my arms expansively.

"I know another big word too." She leaned over me, whispered it in my ear.

She had my full attention again. I was indeed low maintenance. She was incredible.

THE LEAPFROGGING car story was a good example of how she'd do anything for her son.

He was my son too.

The Bobby Swiss thing was something we were having trouble with, though. Lots of trouble. Jeanne was like I had been originally—hoping it would all go away by itself, afraid to mention it.

And although we didn't talk about it much, we thought about it a lot. I could see it in her eyes—something new, mixed with something old. There were moments of silence when I'd glance at her. We both knew.

The more I thought about it—doing dishes in the evening, in the shower in the morning—a strange plan was beginning to form in my head. And unlike Jeanne, I was no genius, so maybe my idea was crazy.

Images and people collided: my father. Jeanne. Adam. Bobby Swiss.

Dayton, Ohio.

II

TV FAMILIES can confuse us. They show kids talking with their parents candidly, discussing problems, relationships, everyone learning valuable life lessons.

It wasn't like that with my parents. My brother and I told them only what they wanted to hear. It took a monumental incident to break down those barriers, to open up with honesty, seek true advice, to pay attention.

In reverse, Mom was better at it than Dad. She liked to talk, to tell us stories of the past. I learned things from her that he would never even allude to. She'd tell us about her mother, her father, her brother, Jack, who disappeared down into the States back in the thirties, the places they lived, family secrets. Details. It was wonderful. Always stories. I couldn't get enough.

"You're special," she'd tell me.

I wanted to be special. I wanted her to tell me why. Often, in the kitchen at Maxwell Avenue, barely old enough to tie my own shoes, I'd coax the same story out of her.

"You've got the Radey blood flowing in your veins. My father told me how the Radeys see things others don't, how they're special."

"Are you special?" I'd ask.

"I must be," she'd say. "I'm a Radey."

"Is Dennis special?"

"Yes."

"Is everyone in the family special?"

"Absolutely."

"Why are we special?"

The pause. The dreamy look. "My father told me that Great-Grampa Radey, who came over from Ireland, had the gift. He said that he could see the past and the future together sometimes."

I loved the dreamy look. It made me feel warm, safe. "Did he see me then?"

She'd meet my eye. "Yes," she'd say. "He saw you. It made him happy."

"Do you see the past and the future together?"

"Not yet," she'd say. "But I will, someday."

I'd wait. I could feel her trying to see it.

"We all will. Someday."

It was in ways like this that her life became an open book, and as I got older, when I became an adult, I saw many of her tales differently, saw how much more she deserved out of life than she ever got.

Dad was a different case. He was tougher. The armor slipped occasionally—like that day his mother was buried. I remember another rare glimpse. I'd seen a name and dates on one of the two family tombstones in Mount Hope—one of many carved there. But this one I didn't recognize.

ANNIE BERTHA NOLAN

BORN JULY 11, 1909–DIED NOVEMBER 29, 1909

I had taken him to the cemetery for a visit. He had asked me to drive him—the kind of day that I usually put off until I ran out of excuses. Standing beside him, I read the inscription. "Who is that?"

"My baby sister."

I knew nothing of this.

"She died when she was four months old." A beat. Another. "It was three days before my fifth birthday."

I turned, watched him stare at the marble monument, his gaze fixed.

"I remember going into my mother's bedroom, seeing her sitting in a chair with the baby in a blanket on her lap. 'She's dead, Tommy,' she said to me."

He stopped suddenly. Neither of us said anything. A

few seconds later, we shuffled our feet in the grass, dug our hands deeper into our pockets.

The moment passed. It was like our brief talk about Bampi. He never spoke of it again. And I never asked. I never heard the story from anyone else in the family.

My cousin, Jacquie, though, did tell me a similar story. It came from her mother, Berna—my father's sister. Jacquie said that her mother told her about a stillborn baby in 1917—eight years after Annie Bertha—whom they kept in a shoebox on the mantle until it was time for burial. This was in the old family house at 222 Berkeley Street, before everyone moved to Maxwell Avenue.

Both these stories came to me after Dad's mother— my grandmother—Nanny, had died. They were details that made me revise how I saw her. Everything we learn helps us revise how we see people.

FATHERS AND sons.

Like my father and me, Adam and I were mostly quiet around each other too.

When I drove him to the Bloor subway line in the morning during school term, we'd talk. A bit. Pretty superficial stuff. Morning's tough to get conversation rolling at the best of times.

He was twenty-one. Just as I had been with my father, there wasn't much he was going to tell me. But it was more complicated than that.

I wasn't his father. Bobby Swiss was.

III

ADAM SHOWED me how to get onto the Internet. The door to his room was open when I passed by and I stopped, stared in. He was at his desk, the computer screen glowing in front of him.

He turned, smiled.

"What's up, sport?"

"Browsing."

I leaned against the doorjamb. "Surfing?" I was showing off. I knew the term.

"C'mere. I'll show you. I'm downloading an article off the Web."

The Web. Magic words to me. Information out of nowhere.

"It's on Madagascar," he said. "Amazing place. Fourth largest island in the world. A micro-continent. It broke off from Africa 125 million years ago and drifted into the Indian Ocean. The people of Madagascar are called the Malagasy."

"This is what you're doing?" My smile mocked him good-naturedly. "When you could be watching TV?"

"Right."

"Where did this all come from?"

"We studied it in anthropology last year."

I'd lost track. "I didn't even know you took anthropology."

"It was one of my options. They make you take options. Try to broaden you."

"Must be awful."

"Terrible." He smiled. "But every now and then some stuff sticks." He looked at me. "Don't tell any of my friends I was doing this on my summer vacation. It wouldn't look good."

"Course not." I frowned. "What would people think?"

"Exactly." He sat back. "What would you like me to find for you, Leo? I'll show you how to use it."

I didn't know. I had to think.

We played around for quite a while before I got rolling, and then I typed in "1960 Chevrolet Impala," my first car, just to see.

"1960 Chev," Adam said. "Jeez. Talk about anthropology. This is a dig. This is archaeology."

The search engine produced a list of them. We visited several sites. Some had them for sale, others listed specs, etc. Fascinating. I saw myself behind the wheel. I saw myself a kid again.

The past: 125 million years or thirty-five years. Bits of it could be retrieved, examined. Once again, I envied Adam his chance at an education—something I had missed.

I saw myself driving that Chev, through Detroit, through Toledo, through Ohio, to Dayton.

DAD'S OLD room needed painting. When Jeanne and I rolled up the rug in there, I saw her pick something up, turn it over, examine it. "What's this?"

It was a tiny wire brush, about three inches long, white bristles at each end. It was bent, twisted. I knew what it was.

"It's used to clean an electric razor."

Jeanne didn't say anything. She handed it to me.

I was kneeling on the floor. I sat back on my heels, held it.

The next morning, the red garnet ring had moved

from the ashtray to the dresser. The razor brush was gone.

He was in the room. He was under the rug. In the tackle box behind the furnace.

I didn't know where he was.

But I knew what I had to do. I couldn't escape it. I knew what I had to do.

IV

THAT YEAR I started my four weeks vacation the last week of July. Jeanne's three weeks wouldn't begin until the first of August. When I told her that I was going to Dayton by myself, she looked at me like I'd lost my mind. "What are you talking about?"

"Three days," I said. "I'll drive. I think I can do it in three days—there and back."

She didn't say anything.

"Maybe four. I'll be back before your holidays."

She shook her head slowly, uncomprehending. Her eyes clouded.

"Four hundred miles or so. I'm guessing."

We were in the kitchen. She sat down, finally stared at me. "What's going on in your head?"

I didn't know what to say. I didn't know how to explain it.

"I have to," I said.

She waited.

"By myself."

She lowered her head, pressed her brow with the palm of her left hand. Slowly, she nodded.

"I've been having dreams," I said.

"I know."

It was my turn to nod. Of course she knew. Then: "I'd like to see Bobby Swiss."

"Oh, Leo."

"Before Adam does."

She looked sad.

"I don't want Adam to get hurt," I said.

"He's twenty-one. He's a big boy."

She was right. "This is for me."

Her eyes deepened. "It was more than twenty years ago, Leo. A lifetime. What are you thinking?"

"It's not that." I shook my head. "It's the dreams." Impossible to explain, I thought.

But Jeanne waited, patient.

"I need to be alone."

The silence expanded. Floating between us, I saw the chipped lamp, the ring, the electric razor. A young man in a Dublin pub. The Greyhound Bus Station in Dayton.

"Alone with my father," I said.

She sat back, looked at me.

"And Adam's."

"This doesn't make any sense."

"I know."

She folded her hands in her lap. "Are you okay, Leo?" The Kentucky drawl that I loved. "Is there anything I can do?"

"I don't think so. I don't know what to tell you. I just have to chase this. It won't go away."

"We're still okay? You and me?"

"We're wonderful."

She smiled.

I wondered how to say it. I wondered how to tell her

that the past had moved inside me, that I had to take it back where it belonged.

"To Dayton?"

I nodded. "To Dayton."

THAT WAS Saturday. I told Adam that I had to go to Cincinnati to see Uncle George, Aunt Amanda's husband, that he needed financial help with his business.

I left Monday morning.

II

The Music

The ancestors come into our homes like guests who need no invitation.

—*Saying of the Malagasy of Madagascar*

Eight

I

DIXIE. THE name conjures up magnolia blossoms, the Deep South. Yet Toronto has a Dixie too—or did have. Just northwest of the city, in what is now suburban sprawl, the village of Dixie sprang up in the early 1800s at the crossroads of Cawthra and Dundas. It wasn't called Dixie immediately. It had to gestate through Fountain Hill, Sydenham, Oniontown, until a local doctor, Beaumont Dixie, donated land for a chapel. Buffalo Bill Cody himself, of Wild West fame, was baptized in that very Dixie Union Chapel. The chapel is still there, but the village is gone, buried beneath strip malls and six lanes of traffic.

In the back of a drawer at home, I have an old receipt, for cemetery plot number 620, in Peace Mount Cemetery, Dixie, Ontario, dated February 21, 1926. It's for the sum of twenty-five dollars, received from Martin Radey.

Martin Radey was my mother's father, my maternal grandfather. He died in 1950. He and his first wife, Maggie, who died in January of 1926, are buried there.

Besides her children, my mother, who died in 1984, has no more living relatives. Her brother, Jack, disappeared back in the thirties. A few summers ago, for the first time, my brother Dennis and I visited plot 620, out of curiosity. There was no monument, no marker of any kind, just a shallow impression in the earth between two other stones. Except for us, no one knows—or cares—that they're there.

On the 401, heading southwest out of Toronto, I passed Dixie Road. It came back to me: my brother and I standing there on the grass, the August sun beating down on us, staring downward, puzzled that no one had ever mentioned that there was no stone, no indicator of any kind.

But they are there. My grandparents. In an unmarked grave. I could feel them as I drove by, off to my right, slightly to the north.

I was going south. Into the past.

SHORTLY BEFORE Windsor, still on the Canadian side, I stopped and had the number six McNuggets Meal at a McDonald's.

THE SIGNS said "Bridge to USA—left," and "Tunnel to USA—right." I went left—up and over. The high road. On the bridge, cars crawling, the afternoon sun was a white-hot light on the Detroit River below.

Traffic stopped. I hung there, suspended, in my 1993 Honda Civic coupe. I pretended I was in my 1960 Chev. The road beneath me vibrated, throbbed, wiggled.

ROUTE 75 South, from Detroit to Toledo: smokestacks, steam, factories. Refinery vats on the right, the Ford plant on the left. Hydro towers marching along beside me for miles, sentinels, four arms spread.

Bob Evans, Super 8. A steady stream of eighteen-wheelers.

Factories gave way to farmland. Flat, nothing. I pulled the visor down to shade my eyes.

Near Monroe, there was a sign that said "Dixie Highway." The past was still with me, everywhere.

Coffee at a Speedway Service Center in Monroe. The place was full of smoke. I dawdled, looked for maps, but they were all out.

"OHIO WELCOMES You to the Heart of It All." The road, which had hummed and clicked evenly from Detroit, smoothed, silent. I was somewhere else, somewhere new. This was different.

TOLEDO HOVERED, a barrier to Ohio.

I saw the first sign for Dayton as I circumvented the city, then a dozen more ("75 South—Dayton") leading me around it, steering me past false exits, distractions, pulling me south. At the tip of Toledo, the three lanes became two, the road simpler. I was being funneled, drawn down purposefully, toward Dayton.

A new sign told me it was 135 miles.

A STRING of geese: a V on the horizon. The bumper sticker ahead: "Pray Hard and Live."

THE SUN fading on my right-hand side.

Exit 181: Bowling Green and Bowling Green State University. I didn't want to drive in the dark. I wanted to see everything.

I took the exit.

II

I DON'T know what made me pull into Bowling Green. I knew it had something to do with the name itself. It was a name I'd heard of. In fact, I even knew there was another one: a Bowling Green, Kentucky. Maybe that was the one I'd heard of. I wasn't sure.

A college town: Burger King, Big Boy, Best Western, Ranch, McDonald's. I drove west along the exit road from 75, on Wooster, past the university, stopped at an unnamed store whose windows were covered with ads for Marlborough Country, Budweiser, Camel, Virginia Slims. I took six cans of Miller High Life from the cooler, paid the girl behind the counter, put them in the trunk of my car, got in and drove back along the route I'd just traveled into town.

I ate dinner at Chi-Chi's. I had the chimichangas and a beer, watched three blond college kids drink margaritas, enjoy a life I had never known.

"WHERE ARE you?"

"Bowling Green, Ohio. I'm in a Days Inn."

A hesitation. "You're okay?"

"I'm fine. I'm even sipping a cold beer."

"Wait a minute. I'll get one. I'll join you."

It was 9 P.M. I smiled, waited. Pictured her running to the fridge. Wondered if I'd been crazy leaving her behind.

She was back. A drink, a sigh. For my benefit. "That's better."

"Isn't this great?"

"About time you called. I've been waiting all evening to have a beer with you."

"What kind have you got?"

"Sleeman's. You?"

"Miller High Life." I studied the can. "The Champagne of Beers."

"Big shot."

"Jet-setter."

We listened to each other breathe, smile.

"Days Inn," she said.

"When I asked them how much it was at the Best Western down the road, they asked if I had AAA membership. I said I did. The price dropped ten percent."

"Very shrewd."

"They never even asked for proof."

"And now, there you are, drinking beer, in the privacy of your very own room."

"A king in his castle."

"You watching dirty movies on the porn station?"

"At a Days Inn? Fat chance. Even if they were here, I couldn't watch them by myself. You'd have to be here with me. I'd get too nuts. What're you doing?"

"Cleaning the house. When you're gone, I clean like a wild woman."

"So the house'll be beautiful when I get back."

"It was beautiful when you left."

"I mean more beautiful."

"That's better. Maybe I'll leave the dishes for you."

"They're mine. Let 'em pile up. I love the dishes."

"Thank God somebody loves them."

"Keep Adam away from them."

"Right."

"Be a shame if he did them."

"Did I hear you say 'fat chance' earlier?"

I took another sip of beer. I could feel her on the other

end. Like I could reach out and touch her. Maybe, I thought, this is phone sex. Without the sex.

"How far are you from Dayton?"

"About two hours, I think. I'll be there before noon tomorrow." Another pause. "I'm right across from Bowling Green State University. It's enormous. I want to look at it a bit in the morning, before I go."

"I wish I were with you."

"You'd be bored."

"With you? Are you kidding? Have you forgotten my traveling bag, all those places, already?"

I was quiet. I hadn't forgotten. I could never forget.

MOUNT AIRY LODGE
"America's Leading Year 'Round Resort"
Mount Pocono, Pennsylvania

MOUNT AIRY LODGE has EVERYTHING!
Ultra-luxury accommodations featuring your
own PRIVATE SWIMMING POOL IN YOUR
ROOM. Heart-shaped Jacuzzi baths and more:

- Indoor and outdoor Olympic-sized heated
  Swimming Pools
- Fabulous Indoor Sports Palace
- Indoor and Outdoor Tennis Courts
- Horseback Riding • Health Club • Marina
- Boating and Sailing on Private Lake
- The "18 Best" P.G.A. Championship Golf Course
- All Winter Sports at our Spectacular Ski Area
- Gourmet Dining and ALWAYS Top-Name
  Entertainment

Write for a brochure:
MOUNT AIRY LODGE, Mount Pocono, PA
Nationwide TOLL-FREE Telephone: 1-800—-

It had been four years earlier, in September—another trip four hundred miles or so. We were veterans of the Niagara Falls Romantic Getaway ("2-night package, Jacuzzi and fireplace suite, walking distance to the Falls"); Niagara was only ninety miles from home. In fact, my grandmother, Nanny, had gone there on her honeymoon with Bampi in 1904. They'd gone in a horse-drawn wagon, one week before her nineteenth birthday. Nanny was three months pregnant with my father.

But we wanted to crank it up a notch. And after Vegas, what was left?

Jeanne heard folks talking about the Pocono Mountains in the cafeteria at work. We had to look them up in our road atlas: northeastern Pennsylvania, eighty miles from Philadelphia, two hours out of New York City.

She got the number through Information, then phoned the Pennsylvania Visitors' Bureau. They flooded us with brochures. We found what we were looking for.

Mount Airy Lodge seemed to be as good as any. The Regency, The Golden Suite, The Villas, The Executive Suite, The Princess Suite, The Monarch Towers, and The Crystal Palace Suite. We booked the most expensive, the most elaborate.

"But we don't need all of that."

"We don't need any of it. This isn't about need."

She looked at me.

"We didn't need Elvis either."

I had her.

It was The Crystal Palace Suite: your own private swimming pool, right in your room. The absolutely essential heart-shaped double Jacuzzi bath. A Swedish sauna and custom-designed shower for two. Log-burning fireplace. The king-sized, round bed. Skylights. Stereo and fridge. And a completely private, outdoor garden courtyard.

Need? What were we talking about?

We took the Friday off work, left early, drove, pulled in late the same day. Friday night and Saturday night. Meals included. We drove home all day Sunday.

Dinners were at an assigned table opposite honeymooners who looked like children to us. The cuisine: upscale airplane food; the service brisk. Live entertainment, dancing: piano, bass, drums. "Memories." "You Are My Hero," "I Just Called to Say I Love You." "Your Momma Don't Sing and Your Daddy Don't Rock and Roll." The announcement of a thirty-eighth birthday, a fiftieth wedding anniversary. Breakfasts were equally curious; beside us: he spoke little English, she didn't care. Both mornings he ate like a man starved, her hands shook from their nightly bacchanalia.

There was no typical couple.

We used every part of our suite, every part of the lodge. We played billiards, took walks, drives, swam naked in our very own pool, sweated in our private sauna, lolled in the heart-shaped tub, ate smoked salmon, cheese, drank Caesars, white wine, red wine, slept when we wanted. And we made love. As often as possible. In every part of our multifaceted nest.

WE'D BEEN trying to get Jeanne pregnant ever since that blinding, sunny day in Las Vegas, when Elvis gave her away, but nothing had happened. And every now and then, when confiding in close friends, we'd hear variations on the same advice:

"You just need to get away. Relax."

"The Greek Isles. You need to go to the Greek Isles."

"Timing. It's all timing."

"It never happens when you want it to. It's always an accident."

"Don't think about it. Just do it."

The Poconos was three years after the wedding in Las Vegas. We were three years older. Time was running out.

Nothing had happened.

Nothing happened in the Poconos either.

III

DAYS INN served the continental breakfast in the lobby: coffee, muffins. While I ate, I read *USA Today* and *The BG News* ("A daily independent student press"). Newspapers were my business; they interested me.

They were my father's business too.

I drove along Wooster, just to have a look. Pretty homes, lovely verandas. BGSU seemed enormous—it stretched its way along into town until I came to Main Street—a real, honest-to-goodness Main Street.

The Cla-Zel Theater, billiards, pizza, Chamber of Commerce.

American Family Insurance, Kirk's Coin Laundry, H & R Block, Huntington Banks.

I pictured Adam going to Bowling Green State University, editing *The BG News*, eating with classmates at Mark's Pub. Maybe this was where he might have ended up if I hadn't entered his life, taken him north. Taken him away from his father.

I got back on I-75, headed south. My eye was drawn

to my hand on the steering wheel, to the red garnet
there.

THE FLAT Ohio countryside continued. Near Findlay, two
cement silos rose up on my left: "Pioneer Sugar."

Only talk shows or static on the radio.

Nine

I

PSYCHOLOGISTS CALL it "Searching Behavior." For the living, it is one way that some deal with grief for the loss of a loved one. I'd read this somewhere, but couldn't remember where.

I think it's simpler than that. I think there are family ghosts. I think they are something real and powerful that we carry inside us, that without them we're empty, without direction. They steer us, advise us, converse with us daily.

They bring the past and the present together. Give us a future, a perspective. They humble us.

AT EXIT 161: the University of Findlay. Exit 145: Ohio Northern University. Exit 142: Bluffton College.

Adam could be studying at any of them. Findlay and Lima must have newspapers where I could work. Or the *Dayton Daily News*. It was possible.

NEAR LIMA: Comfort Inn, Days Inn. "United States Plastic." Beside it: "Christ Is the Answer."

I crossed the Ottawa River, thought of Canada's capital. Like Dixie, my world and the past had come with me, clinging, recurring like distant speed bumps.

—◆—

OHIO STATE University, Lima Campus, off to the east. A woman hanging wash on a line.

Flat. Cows. The sun came down in actual rays through the clouds: like a postcard.

I was thirsty. The juice machine back in the Bowling Green Days Inn lobby had been out of order.

Economy Inn, Hampton Inn, The Olive Garden—all visible from the highway.

EXIT 111: the Neil Armstrong Air and Space Museum. The sign said, "75 South—Dayton." Again. There was no doubt where I was going.

AT PIQUA, Exit 83: "Paul Sherry RV's, Ohio's Largest Dealer, 350 + New Ones & Used." Red Carpet Inn. Edison Community College.

The giant Panasonic factory on my right, near Troy.

Dayton, eighteen miles.

I thought of Adam and the three blond students I'd seen at Chi-Chi's in Bowling Green, thought of them in residence at the bucolic campus there, of how different his life was compared to theirs.

NEAR TIPP City, south of Troy, the road flared to three lanes. The chain restaurants resurfaced: Red Lobster, Bob's Crab Shack, Outback, Bob Evans.

Then, DAYTON CORP LIMIT.

Bobby Swiss. Adam. Jeanne. Everybody was there with me. My father was there. Even Aidan, my stillborn son.

II

NANNY—MY paternal grandmother—was born June 15, 1885. She died December 27, 1974. Her maiden name was Annie Sutton. She was baptized at St. Mary's Church, on Bathurst Street, in Toronto.

Because she lived at Maxwell with my parents, a lot of the trivia of her life fell into my father's hands when she passed away. And now it's fallen into mine. That's how I know her dates, her place of baptism. I've got her birth certificate and her death certificate.

I also came across three postcards from France.

July 28, 1917

Dear Father

Just a card to let you know I am well and hope you and mother are in the best of health I received 2 letters from you dated June 24 and July 1 and am glad to hear you are well I will write a letter later on for I know you like to hear from me often so cheer up good days coming when we meet I remain your loving son HMS XXXXXXXXXX

September 13, 1917

Dear Mother

Just a card to let you know I am always thinking of you and hope you and father are in the best of health as it don't leave me so bad for I am picking up again I remain your loving son somewhere in france do my bit XXXXX XXXXXXX

September 24, 1917

Dear Father

Just a line to let you know I received your letter ok and glad to hear you and mother are well as it leaves me getting on well after the shell shock I got but my nerves are a little shaky yet but will come around alright the Dr. said I remain your son HMS XXXXX

Not exactly French postcards as I understood the term.

Since Dad's death, my cousin Jacquie was the oldest in the family, so I asked her. "Who are they from?"

"Uncle Mike. He was Nanny's brother. He was adopted. He was in the war. He was shell-shocked. He was never right afterward."

All news to me.

"I've got an old picture of Da and Jim, standing outside 222 Berkeley Street in 1918. The house is decorated with streamers and flags. There's a big sign across the top of the veranda that says 'Welcome Home.' It was all for Mike."

"Did Nanny have any other brothers or sisters?"

"No. She was an only child, so Da and her mother adopted Mike. That way they had a boy and a girl."

"Two of them are signed 'HMS.' What's that? His Majesty's Service, because he was a soldier?"

"His name was Henry. Henry Michael Sutton. But he was always Uncle Mike."

Henry Sutton. That was the name of the godfather on the baptismal certificate of Dad's that I'd come across— the one in that brown leather folder that he kept in the top drawer of his dresser. A person to go with the name. A new sprig of foliage on the tree.

"What happened to him? To Mike?"

"He married Agnes after the war. Marie Agnes. Aunt Aggie. They had two boys—Tommy and Jimmy Sutton. Tommy joined the Christian Brothers and became Brother Julian. He died just after World War Two. A urinary tract infection. He was only twenty-four. Jimmy joined the paratroopers. He moved out west. Edmonton, I think. He had a son who became an Anglican minister."

Tributaries, with small rills trickling off. I could hear them, bubbling, like streams down a mountainside.

"During the Depression, Mike couldn't get a job. He used to take a shovel and go line up somewhere downtown with the unemployed, waiting for work. He didn't have the carfare to get there. Nanny used to give him a ticket."

"What happened to him?"

"He died."

"When?"

"I don't know. Agnes died first. He married again."

"Where are they buried?"

"I don't know." A sigh. "I'm sorry, Leo. I haven't thought about them in years. I don't know what happened to any of them."

DA HAD wanted a son, so he had adopted Mike. My Uncle Jim, like Da, had wanted a son. In my mother's story, he would have even taken me. He had adopted two sons.

Ghosts are real. They don't need our belief. They exist because struggle and failure have value. They slow down time, let us move backward.

They had traveled here with me, through Ohio, to Dayton. In my 1960 Chev.

DAYTON. MAIN Street.

There it was again. Everywhere.

It seemed as good a bet as any. I turned off.

Left: downtown. Over the river. Stop at the traffic lights at Monument Avenue.

Interstate Mortgage Company, Fifth Third Bank, National City Bank. I was in a financial district.

The Dayton Convention Center at Fifth and Main.

I pulled over in front of Otis Elevator to orient myself.

I turned back, went east along Fifth.

There it was: the red, white, and blue striped logo of the Greyhound Bus Station, from my dream.

At St. Clair—another name from Toronto, from the past—I pulled into an Arby's parking lot, stayed in the car, pulled out my map of Dayton, saw where I was. Looking up through the windshield: Hauer Music Company. To the left, a building with the windows broken, slated for demolition. Slated into memory only. Like the Hacienda Hotel in Las Vegas.

I reached into my shirt pocket, took out the address and phone number. I looked at it.

ARBY'S DIDN'T appeal. Not enough hunger yet. Where I wanted to go was south through the city. Southeast, actually. A suburb called Kettering.

Past Miami Valley Hospital on Main, the road changed. Suddenly, for the first time in what seemed to be hundreds of miles, I saw hills, trees, and the landscape became small-town pretty. Oakwood: a bandstand—a gazebo—in a park at Shantz. The road wound upward. Somewhere Main had become Far Hills.

Arrow Wine and Spirits. Lincoln Park Medical Center.

Kettering City Schools Board of Education building.

I was close.

At Stroop Road, I pulled into the Town and Country

Shopping Center. I was finally hungry. For lunch, I treated myself to New Orleans–style crabcakes and seafood chowder at the Peasant Stock Restaurant.

III

EAST ALONG Stroop to Woodman, north to Dorothy Lane, then east again to Galewood. At the Midas Muffler on Dorothy, near the tail end of Woodlane Plaza, I pulled in, took the slip of paper from my pocket, read it: *Bobby Swiss, 2926 Galewood Street*, and the phone number.

It was 2 P.M.

Midas advertised Lube & Oil, Brakes, Pipes, Mufflers, Shocks & Struts. Nobody came out, nobody bothered me.

I drove across Dorothy Lane, up Galewood.

THE ADDRESS was a small, white, wooden bungalow on my right, with a door in the center. It probably had two bedrooms. I continued driving, mesmerized, till Ghent Avenue, turned left, another left at Acosta, then back along Galewood for another look. I did it again. And once more.

I was here, at last.

A WORKING-CLASS neighborhood. Blue-collar. Neat, clean. Real estate had a name for homes like these: starter home, empty-nester.

It was the middle of the afternoon. I parked down the block, pulled on my ivy cap and sunglasses, got out, wandered up the street. Opposite the house was a park set up for kids, backing onto a complex that included a Montessori School, Baptist Center, Ballet School.

I found a bench in the park, behind a swing set and

sandbox, sat down, stretched my arms along its back, pulled the cap down low over my eyes, let the sun beat down.

I sat there for an hour, staring at the house, then I left.

ON 675 North, I drove until the usual signs appeared, near Fairborn: Holiday Inn, Fairfield Inn, Homewood Suites, Hampton Inn. Bob Evans, McDonald's, Arby's, Wendy's.

I ate dinner at Chi-Chi's. I had the chimichangas and a beer. It had been good in Bowling Green, it was still good here.

The Hampton Inn that I checked into was on Presidential Avenue, off John Glenn Parkway, right opposite Wright State University. Standing in my room, looking out the window, I pictured Adam going there, carrying his books across the broad campus, living in Dayton, with his father.

Ten

I

I DREAMED that night of my father flying in on a plane to meet me. At the airport, I told him that I didn't like looking after his money, that I didn't want the responsibility. As in other dreams, he was young. His hair had blond streaks in it—which, if you'd seen my father, made no sense at all.

He told me that young people are always angry, that when I was older, more damaged, I'd understand.

The dream was already fading as I stepped out of my morning shower. Sitting on the edge of the bed, studying the map of Dayton, I realized that it had disappeared down drains, into the rivers around the city—the Greater Miami, Wolf Creek, the Stillwater. Mad River.

MAD RIVER.

During the last six months of his life, Dad suffered from dementia. It was triggered by the first of the two bouts of pneumonia that finished him. It was explained to me that pneumonia in the elderly can act like a stroke, cutting off necessary oxygen to the brain.

There were moments of lucidity, mingled with the madness. One day, sitting in the green, cloth-covered chair in his room, five days before he died, he talked.

"I'm near the end. I know that." Pause. "If you move over to the other side of the plane, there are better seats. I was in Hamilton yesterday. Today I was in Kingston." The eyes, watery. "I slept with a woman last night. She was a big woman, bigger than that nurse who used to come to see me." Struggling. A frown. Then: "I dream a lot now. I don't know when I'm dreaming and when I'm not."

I listened.

I'D PHONED Jeanne before I went to bed the previous night.

"Tonight?"

"Hampton Inn."

"Big spender. What's Dayton like?"

"Don't know yet."

"You must have some impression."

I thought about it, about the Convention Center, Otis Elevator, the Greyhound Bus Station, the building near Arby's, boarded up, ready for demolition. I thought about Oakwood, the gazebo, hills, trees, the Peasant Stock Restaurant in the mall. "You can't pigeonhole it. I saw a business section, some inner-city stuff. Then you drive farther, there's a beautiful suburb, big houses. It's like you. Too complex."

We sipped our beers, four hundred miles apart.

"So I'm complex, huh?"

"Isn't complex good?"

"How am I complex?"

"You're always planning ahead. You're smarter than me."

"How could anyone be smarter than you?"

"Touché."

"One example. Just one."

"You taught me how to shop, how to plan. Buy bulk.

Like the running shoes on sale, you bought two pairs, put one in the closet. I only bought the one pair. Two years later, you whip out your second pair, toss the old away. Me, I had to go shopping again. Like a dumbhead."

"I got 'em on right now."

"I know you do."

"How do you know?"

"You wear them when you're cleaning. You're cleaning, aren't you? Like a wild woman?"

"Maybe you're wrong. Maybe I'm stark naked."

"Maybe you are."

"Think about it."

"I am." And I did. But not for long. I knew I'd never sleep.

We listened to each other breathe over the phone. It was comforting. She never asked the questions she wanted to ask, and I was grateful, because I didn't know any of the answers.

DA, MY father's maternal grandfather, my great-grandfather—whose name was Thomas Samuel Sutton—was an imposing figure. On a wall in his room my father kept a black-and-white photograph in a twelve-by-fourteen-inch frame of my brother Ron, circa 1934, at about two years of age, sitting on Da's knee. It's a handsome photo—done in a studio. If I were guessing, I'd say Da paid for it. He looks pretty proud.

Ron is wearing a sailor suit. Da has on a three-piece suit and a bow tie. My father has Da's ears, the long lobes. He has his mouth.

If Nanny was the matriarch of my memory, Da was the patriarch of the previous generation. My father must have lived in his shadow. Certainly Bampi—Dad's father—

107

did. There are some good stories of Da still circulating through the family. I've heard them. Jacquie has told me most of them.

Da couldn't read or write. He used to get one of the kids around the house to read the newspaper to him. He spent time in the backyard, the garden, the garage of the house on Maxwell Avenue. When I was a kid we could still see some of the harps that he had carved into the side of the garage. He was born in Toronto in 1862. His father, Sam Sutton, was born in Dublin in 1842. Once, in the early 1930s, he raised the Irish flag on a pole from that garage. Someone complained. The police came and made him take it down.

Among my father's things I also found a receipt, dated October 21, 1899: *Received from Mr. Thomas Sutton, the sum of $951.46, payment in full for 81 Duke Street, Toronto . . . signed, Annie Russell, Executrix.* Duke Street no longer exists. It's been blended into Adelaide Street. The house is long gone too.

Da, son of Sam Sutton of Dublin, both illiterate laborers, had managed to accumulate enough cash to buy a house, something even I couldn't do. He gave us all a leg up, a small start. It was a beginning. We stood on his shoulders.

In the photo, my brother Ron's hands are resting on his great-grandfather's. Ron told me once that Da used to take him out on Sunday afternoons for a walk, a ride on the streetcar, then to a playground. This would have been around 1937. Ron would have been about five years old. Inevitably, they would visit a bootlegger and Da would have a drink. When they got home, Nanny would be suspicious and grill Ron with questions. He'd always answer that he didn't know where they went. Sitting in the corner of the kitchen, Da would beam, a twinkle in his eye, say That's my boy, That's my boy. We'll go for walks and rides to the playground every Sunday.

Da, Thomas Sutton, was a widower from 1930 until he died in 1944. He lived at Maxwell Avenue for those fourteen years. I think he needed that drink on Sunday afternoons.

Ron died May 23, 1993, age sixty.

IT WAS 5 A.M. I had no idea what Bobby Swiss did for a living, what time he got up, where he went, if he even went anywhere. I wanted to be sure that I didn't miss him.

Coffee, orange juice, muffin, and strawberry yogurt in the Hampton Inn lobby, another coffee to go, then back onto 675 South. Within twenty minutes, I was in my car, parked on Galewood, watching the house where he lived. The steam from my coffee made a crescent on the windshield. The paper cup warmed my hands. I squinted into the summer sun, rising in the east, behind the house

AT SIX-THIRTY, he came out. I knew it was him. He wore jeans, a white T-shirt, had a cigarette in his mouth. Tall, strong, his hair shoulder-length, brown, combed back behind his ears. He hadn't shaved. The rhythm of his body, the way he walked: I realized who I was seeing. I was seeing Adam.

He got into the '87 Olds parked in the driveway. When it pulled out, I saw the license plate: JESUSROX. I started up my car, followed the early morning exhaust cloud north on Galewood.

Galewood curved west, became Bingham. At Woodman Drive—Wright Brothers Parkway—he turned left, driving along the perimeter of a classic factory, the Delco

Plant: acres of parking behind wire fencing, thousands of cars. Smokestacks, gray vats, electrical transformers.

He turned right, into the entrance driveway—a long, wide road leading into the grounds—stopped at the gatehouse, said something, then was gone. I pulled over at the foot of the entranceway, sat for a minute more, then drove away.

II

DAD ATTENDED grade school at St. Paul's Catholic Elementary School on Sackville, near Parliament and Queen. Born in 1904, he was there from 1910 to 1918—eight years that were the extent of his formal education. At age fourteen, he went to work.

He told me the Christian Brothers taught him. The boys and girls were in separate classes, played on separate sides of the school grounds at recess. He said Brother Jerome, his eighth-grade teacher, could plunk an eraser off a kid's head from thirty feet, a trick that was held in high esteem by his students. No one complained to their parents. If they did, they got whapped again. You must have deserved it, they were told.

He was an altar boy, serving Sunday Mass at St. Paul's Church, across from the school. The image of my father as a kid in grade school is hard enough for me to conjure up. The thought of him as an altar boy is almost incomprehensible.

The whole area was called Cabbagetown. Irish Cabbagetown. Up until the 1950s it was pretty much a slum. Today, it's quite gentrified, diverse, interesting, downtown, central—trendiness mingled with vestigial traces of the old, the seedy. Corktown was a part of it—the part south of Queen, where St. Paul's was. Quite appropriate, since Dad's paternal grandfather, a shoemaker by trade, one of my great-grandfathers—who had the same name as Dad's father, Matthew Nolan—was born in County Cork, Ireland, in 1842.

It was in the newspaper just recently: six coffins discovered during playground construction at St. Paul's School, which was built upon a nineteenth-century cemetery. Burial records show that nearly three thousand Catholics were interred there between 1847 and 1857. No one knows how many bodies were buried between 1822, when it opened, and 1847, when records began. Thousands more, presumably. Also in the area is a mass trench, containing more than eight hundred Catholics who died of typhus in 1847—emigrants who had escaped the Irish famine only to perish thousands of miles away, be buried in that strange, hard soil. The cemetery was closed in 1857 because it was full; grave markers—not the bodies—were removed in 1870.

As a child, my father played atop their bodies. Brother Jerome wielded his eraser there. They are still there, an entire community, founders, shoring us up, unsung.

My father and Brother Jerome are still there too.

JEANNE: *He told her he was working in a factory in Dayton. That's how I know what I know.*

Delco. It fit. Owned by General Motors. Jesus. I even had a Delco battery keeping the electrics in my '93 Honda Civic humming. I saw the irony: maybe Bobby Swiss had made the unit that helped power me here, to Dayton, across Mad River, to this low floodplain of the Great Miami, seat of Montgomery County.

Down a funnel. Inevitable.

—⁓⁓—

MY MAP told me I was actually in Kettering. From what I could determine, Dayton was a metropolitan area that included the cities of Kettering, Miamisburg, Xenia, Fairborn, Oakwood, and Vandalia. Population of Dayton was around two hundred thousand. If you included the greater metropolitan area, it went up around a million.

I stopped at a 7-Eleven, looked up Delco in the phone book, and called. I told the woman who answered that I was a journalist doing an article on factory shift work, and asked them how long a typical shift would be at their plant. The one that starts at 7 A.M., for instance.

"It finishes at five. Shifts are eight hours, with an hour for lunch or dinner, and two half-hour breaks."

I hung up. I had a whole day ahead of me. I bought a pocket guide to Dayton.

I'D SEEN Wright State University from my window at the Hampton Inn. Like Bowling Green, I wanted to see more of it.

IT WAS enormous, a huge campus. And beautiful: trees, ravines. I parked the car, got out, walked for a bit.

My guide told me that its charter was less than thirty years old, that there were sixteen thousand students here, more than ninety percent of them Ohioans, that there were seven hundred thousand volumes in the libraries. As a state university, its tuition was around four thousand dollars—double that if you were from out of state—staggering sums to me, especially when you factored in living expenses as well.

In the bookstore, Dayton's aviation pioneers, Orville

and Wilbur Wright, were represented by a silhouetted logo of their famous biplane. A metaphor for discovery, change, literally throwing off earthly shackles, defying gravity, they had taken flight, freed themselves.

As at Bowling Green, and as I had the previous evening from the window of my room at the Hampton Inn, I pictured Adam sitting in libraries here, surrounded by seven hundred thousand books, studying in the state where he was born.

Research, books, community service, the arts and sciences—opportunities engulfing these people in their green and gold sweatshirts, under the bright Ohio sun.

In my mind, Adam and I became one. I was attending classes with him. If I had gone to university, would I have been smart enough to understand what was happening to me? Was there a way to learn what I wanted to know, especially when I wasn't even certain what it was that I wanted to know?

I envied Adam his life. I envied him that he still had a father.

IT WAS 10 A.M., was warming to a hot, clear day.

In the night all things were possible, anything could happen. The dreams had proven this to me. Things changed, ever so subtly, every time I awoke. The world shifted, in fractions, the past and the present existing together, inside me. My mind roamed free.

The sun beating down changed all that.

The booklet in my hip pocket told me that Kettering, where Bobby Swiss lived and worked, was named after Charles F. Kettering, who, along with Edward Deeds, developed the modern automotive starter and ignition systems.

I sat in my Honda, keys in hand. I looked out through the windshield into the glare of morning, tried to will the night magic to appear. I inserted the key into Kettering's ignition, turned it, heard the Delco battery fire the noisy valves of my 1960 Chev to life. I closed my eyes, saw the shaky three-speed gearshift on the steering column, felt its wide bench seat beneath me.

Eleven

I

WEST OF 675, off Shakertown Road, just outside Kettering, I saw the Belmont Auto Theatre.

$6.00 A CARLOAD

OPEN WEEKENDS

THROUGHOUT THE WINTER
HEATERS WILL BE FURNISHED
FOR YOUR COMFORT

NO ALCOHOL
ON THIS
PROPERTY

I got out of the car, stood with my hands in my pockets. Then I went up to the fence and peered through.

I KNOW a lot about drive-in theaters. I've made it a point to find out. I like them. I bought a book about them once—written by some guy who had taken a trip along Route 66, searching them out. He liked them even more than I did. I'll tell you a little bit of what I know.

By the early thirties, Detroit was rolling cars off the assembly line, Hollywood was churning out movies. The first drive-in opened in New Jersey in 1933, an unexpected offshoot of the two growing industries. Over the next decade drive-in theaters began to appear all over the States: Pennsylvania, Texas, California, Massachusetts, Florida, Maine, Michigan, Rhode Island, New York. By 1942, there were ninety-five of them, scattered across twenty-seven states.

As I recall, Ohio took the concept to its bosom: it had more than any other state. Eleven, I think. Like the one I was looking at right now. Good old Ohio.

During 1941–45, the War years, for all the obvious reasons the whole phenomenon flattened out. But it blossomed again with a vengeance after the War. Before 1950, their number had increased from around one hundred to over eight hundred. By 1958, there were close to five thousand.

And the one near Copiague, New York, on Long Island, almost overlooking South Oyster Bay and Ocean Parkway—that was one of the largest, one I wanted to get to, but never did. It hosted twenty-five hundred cars, had an additional twelve-hundred-seat, heated and air-conditioned indoor viewing area, playground, cafeteria, and restaurant with full dinners. A shuttle train took the moviegoers from their cars to the various destinations on the twenty-eight-acre site. I also heard of one in Lufkin, Texas, and another in Troy, Michigan, both of which claimed parking space for three thousand vehicles.

Onward and upward, fun and novelty for everyone, unlimited expansion. Playgrounds might incorporate minitrains, boat and pony rides, talent and animal shows, even miniature golf. Fried chicken, burgers, pizza: fast food was a natural.

In the 1960s and seventies, the party wasn't quite over, but it was ending. The numbers leveled, the enthusiasm waned. By the end of the eighties, they were closing with regularity. Suburban ones were engulfed by housing and shopping developments, their property too valuable. Many of the rural ones just withered and died. There are close to a thousand dead drive-ins across the U.S., weeds sprouting freely—graveyards, the speaker posts like headstones.

The States has fewer than a thousand left. Canada has about seventy-five.

The drive-in theater. Although you can find one in most countries on the globe, they're a particularly American hybrid. Passion pits for teens, cheap entertainment for families. Young couples with an infant could avoid the hassle of a baby-sitter—just plunk junior in the backseat with a bottle, let him sleep.

Yet what was its life span? Seventy years? Eighty? Like a person's: birth, development, excitement, expansion, settling, then decline.

WHEN I was a kid in the 1950s, I always wanted my parents to take me to a drive-in movie. It never happened. They would just chuckle when I mentioned it. It wasn't something they could relate to. I guess there's no better way to build an obsession.

The first one I ever managed to get to was with my older cousin Jo-Anne—Eleanor's daughter—and her boyfriend (later husband) Bob. They were teens and my brother Dennis and I were six and eleven. It was summer vacation, near Bancroft, Ontario, some 160 miles northeast of Toronto, where Jo-Anne and Bob lived. Just outside of town, you turned off at Bird's Creek, onto a dirt road.

The Bancroft Drive-In. I loved it—a horror double bill. On a hot July night, Dennis and I sat in the dark, in the backseat of Bob's car, enthralled.

Last summer, when Jeanne and I were visiting a friend who has a cottage in the area, I detoured down that road just to have a look. The road is paved now, and there's no sign of the drive-in theater. It's gone. Vanished. Not abandoned or grown over, just gone. Houses line the road. After more than forty years, I couldn't even determine where exactly it had been. I even wondered if I'd imagined the whole thing.

But I didn't. It's still there. I know it is. Like my '60 Chev, like everything else that ever existed, it's all there. Because it happened. Because I was there. Because it's inside me.

I REMEMBER a summer evening in my teens, cruising around Toronto in my father's car with my buddy, Joe. We ended up on Kennedy Road, north of Eglinton, near the Scarboro Drive-In.

Summer '61. I was seventeen. Mantle and Maris each had thirty-five home runs by mid-July, and Ford Frick, Commissioner of Baseball, ruled that for either of them to beat Ruth's record of sixty, they had to do it in 154 games, instead of the new, expanded 162-game schedule. Gus Grissom was pulled from his Mercury capsule *The Liberty Bell* in the Atlantic near Grand Bahama Island, just before it sank three miles to the ocean floor. The baseball Leafs were probably playing the Buffalo Bisons down at the old stadium near the foot of Bathurst. I think that was also the summer that Cupcakes Cassidy was at the Casino ("Tops in Variety and Burlesque") at Queen and Bay.

If I'd stayed home on a Saturday night, I'd end up sitting with family—Mom, Dad, Nanny, maybe Dennis too—all compromising on acceptable fare on the RCA black-and-white: *Gunsmoke* at eight; *Lawrence Welk* at nine. My only hope was talking them into switching from good old Lawrence at nine-thirty to *Have Gun Will Travel*. Now that wasn't bad.

Anyway, the Scarboro Drive-In while cruising. *From the Terrace* was playing. Adult entertainment. I don't remember the second feature.

We didn't drive the car in. We parked it on a dirt road and went in on foot, across fields, through ditches, over a barbed-wire fence—all in the dark.

I remember my feet were soaked, that Joe fell on his back, his leg hooked onto the barbed wire, that even as we were doing it, we knew it was insane.

Why did we do it? Because we were seventeen. It was wonderful.

That was my second time at a drive-in. Under the summer stars, beside a speaker post at the rear of the lot, we sat down on the grass, ate popcorn from the concession booth, and watched Paul Newman and Joanne Woodward.

II

AFTER I got my own car, the Chev, I tried taking girls a few times. The North-East. The Dufferin, the Scarboro, the 400, the 7&27. Most of my dates thought it was kitschy the first time, but I can't recall any enthusiasm for a second visit. I took Fran, my first wife, once. She didn't like it. I began to think I was the only one who liked them.

I gave them up for years. Until Jeanne. She liked them. Adam liked them. We had fun.

By then, there were only two left: the 400 and 7&27. Now, they're both gone too.

"DID YOU ever go to the drive-in back home?" The first time I asked her, we were driving down the 400 into the city. You could see the multiscreen complex off to the west.

"Yeah, I went, lots. The Trail Drive-In, about a mile south of Ashland, on Route 60. Right near Crisp's hot dog stand. Crisp's had apple turnovers with powdered sugar and ice cream. Good eatin'. If we didn't go to Crisp's, we'd hit the Bluegrass Grill on Winchester. Get a hot dog and a root beer, or one of their Flying Saucer Burgers, with the special sauce." A smile. "The Trail's gone now. Wollohan's Home Improvements is there." She toyed with her hair, that way she has. "There were others. Flatwoods had a drive-in—The Corral, across from Espy Road. Another one in Summit. Huntington had one—called The East. Had a rising sun on it. I think it's still there. The others, though, like The Trail, they're all gone too." She was remembering more. "Sometimes we'd go farther, make an evening out of it, maybe even a night. But that was part of the fun."

I brightened. "Where'd you go?"

"Across the river, into Ohio. The Kanauga, near Gallipolis. Route 7 North, on the Ohio River. About thirty miles." She was warming to it. "Bunch of us kids from Ashland might go in a couple of cars. Sometimes, a lot of the boys would hide in the trunk and we'd sneak them in. That was part of the fun too."

"Ever get caught?"

"Nope. Place was started up by a local family after the War—passed down through generations. It's still family owned and operated. Lot of 'em are. We think they knew, but didn't care. I remember Monday night was Carload Night."

"Most women I've met haven't liked drive-ins," I said. "You like 'em?"

I nodded. "Love 'em."

"Well, fella," she said, "this is your lucky day."

I looked at her, at the smile.

"Again," she said.

"OTHERS WERE near Lexington: Mount Sterling, Paris, Stanton, Winchester. Went to the one near Mount Sterling a couple of times, but that was pretty far. Must have been a hundred miles. Besides the Kanauga, we tried the Scioto Breeze, outside Lucasville, north of Portsmouth. Another one near Jackson, Ohio. And one in West Virginia—on Route 35 at St. Albans. That's near Charleston. It's closed now. I heard they turned it into a lumberyard."

I stopped and looked at her.

"Yeah?" She tossed the hair from her face.

"Amazing."

"What is?"

I shook my head. "I never thought I'd find you."

THAT SUMMER, 1989, after a trip to Boston, on our way back through New York State, we dawdled, enjoyed the drive. Around dinnertime, we pulled off I-90 through East Greenbush, outside Albany, and looked for a place to stay for the night. At the Econo Lodge in Rensselaer, I got out, went inside, and asked the girl at the desk how much.

"Fifty-four ninety-five. Unless you want the upgrade. It's got a fridge, coffeemaker, hair dryer . . ."

"How much?"

"Fifty-nine ninety-five."

"Upgrade me." She didn't know who she was dealing with.

I saw it while browsing through brochures and a local newspaper, sitting on the bed in our fabulous room, looking for a place to eat. Jeanne was studying the hair dryer. "The Hollywood Drive-In," I said.

She turned.

"Route 66, Averill Park Road, just east of Albany." I looked up.

A smile. "What's playing?"

I shrugged. "Who cares?"

DINNER: AT the concession stand, pizza was seven dollars. With pepperoni, it was eight. We ordered it with. After all, I was a guy who had an upgraded room at the Econo Lodge.

We parked in a rear corner, ate in the car, trying not to get tomato sauce all over ourselves in the dark. Drive-in movies tend not to be first run. The first feature was *Rain Man*. It had already won the Academy Award, back in March. Great movie. Men after my own heart, going to Vegas, winning just enough to solve a problem, no more. My dream.

Jeanne came back from the washroom at intermission. "You have to see that one to believe it. I had to line up outside there were so many of us. One woman actually butted in. I let her. I tried to imagine having to go to the bathroom that bad."

"I understand. I saw the men's."

Second feature was *Funny Farm* with Chevy Chase. It was a good one to miss. As well as she could with the stick shift between us, Jeanne nestled in my arm. "You ever make out at the drive-in?"

"Is that a question you'd like me to ask you?"

She moved slightly. Closer. "I guess not."

I answered anyway. "A bit. More ambition than success. Callow youth."

She kissed my neck. "How 'bout now?"

There were only about a hundred cars in a lot that could hold three hundred. There was nobody near us. The window was rolled down halfway. Crickets, the stars, the smell of a summer night in the country.

"It's a good time," she said.

For a minute, I didn't follow.

"Middle of the month."

A slow dawning.

"And lots of girls get pregnant in the backseat of an automobile."

Suddenly I wasn't forty-five years old. I was eighteen. We locked the doors, got into the backseat of the Honda, pushed the front seats as far ahead as they'd go.

"You gotta admit," she said, "it's a perfect spot."

"It's a perfect idea."

And we made love. I won't tell you how we did it. I'll let you imagine. But we did it. It was a tribute to our ingenuity. And it was great. In fact, it was incredible.

NEXT MORNING, I had coffee, juice, and the Grand Slam breakfast at Denny's. Jeanne had the Ham 'N' Chedda Omelet.

Talk about celebrating.

III

THE FINGER Lakes—Seneca, Cayuga, Owasco, and others—are southeast of Rochester, southwest of Syracuse, maybe two hundred miles farther on from our upgraded Econo Lodge quarters. They were only a small detour on the way home, and worth seeing. This time we cranked it up a notch again—to the Holiday Inn in Auburn. $89. We were still celebrating.

In McMurphy's Pub, downstairs, we sat at the bar and ordered the clam chowder and pints of Guinness for dinner. After eating chili dogs, fries, yogurt smoothies, and Mrs. Field's cookies at rest stops all the way along I-90, it was all we wanted. Besides, we were too impatient. We were on a mission.

The Finger Lakes Drive-In was on Route 20, just west of Auburn. We'd spotted it late in the afternoon, touring around.

BULL DURHAM was a wonderful movie: sexy, smart, funny. We'd seen it last winter, but it was even better now.

"What do you think of Susan Sarandon?" asked Jeanne.

"Can't hold a candle to you. You'd have to give her lessons."

"Good answer."

"Getting better, aren't I?"

"There's hope."

Picture a wooden box office, wooden concession booth, that giant screen, a sloping field of soft grass, a handful of scattered automobiles, that summer smell. It was a clear, dark evening. Stars like diamonds, enough to make you ache.

We rolled up the windows against mosquitoes, locked the doors, climbed into the backseat, and gave *"Crocodile" Dundee II* a miss.

A movie with a Roman numeral in its title, about an Australian who hunted crocodiles. How could we relate?

NEXT MORNING, at the Auburn Family Restaurant, I had eggs, bacon, home fries, toast, juice, and coffee. Jeanne had the same, but substituted sausages for the bacon.

What can I say? Celebration after celebration. When you're happy, you're happy.

IN TORONTO, we went back to work, back to routines with Adam. Jeanne's cycle came and went. I think that was when I started to have some of my night sweats, started to wonder, before I started putting any of the pieces together.

Like Las Vegas, the Poconos, like Niagara Falls before that, nothing happened.

IV

OUTSIDE THE Belmont Auto Theater near Dayton, in the bright sunshine, I got back into my car.

Twelve

I

FROM 675, I drove east out of Dayton along the Yellow Springs Road. A mile farther, near Byron, there were cattle. Suddenly I was in the country. Just as suddenly: a pretty road, lovely homes, horses. Landscaping, three-car garages. Farms.

Within minutes, Yellow Springs, population 4,600. The main street was artsy, attractive. Ye Olde Trail Tavern Restaurant. Dino's Cappuccinos. Ohio Silver Company. I drove past the Little Art Theater too quickly to notice what was playing.

Then Antioch College. I got out my pocket guide, looked through it: 325,000 volumes in the Olive Kettering Library; student newspaper: *Antioch Record*.

A small college. Expensive.

Adam couldn't afford it. I couldn't afford to send him. From what I had seen, neither could his father.

I got out of the car, stood on the lawn beside the college sign, stared at the oaks, the maples, the building beyond them with its six spires.

IN THE house on Maxwell Avenue, we had a small liquor cabinet in the dining room when I was growing up. It was about two feet square, with hinged doors that swung from its middle, and a drawer at the bottom. Inside, in one half were shelves, filled with an assortment of different-sized tumblers for various concoctions; the other half was a space for standing bottles. There were never any bottles. Nobody in my family was a wine drinker. And none of them could handle hard liquor, so there was seldom any in the house. Beer was often plentiful—especially on week-ends—but was kept in the fridge or in the cool darkness beneath the stairs in the back kitchen, en route to the basement.

Hard liquor was drunk in bars and cocktail lounges, outside the home, on rare occasions. A souvenir of such momentous episodes was the plastic swizzle stick accompanying the drink. The drawer at the bottom of the liquor cabinet contained dozens. As kids, we could play for hours in that drawer, building with them (more interesting than Lego), lining them up, trading them, organizing by colors, shapes. There were arrows, feathers, sabers, spears, flags. No one minded us on the floor with them; we were quiet.

When I was between the ages of ten and twelve Nanny took me with her on her annual week's summer vacation to Buffalo. Previously, she'd always gone by herself. The first year we took the bus, the next the train, and finally we flew. Nanny had never been on an airplane, and wanted to try it. It was my first flight too. We couldn't have been in the air more than twenty minutes. It was ninety miles by road, sixty by air across Lake Ontario. On the last trip, she was seventy years old.

We stayed in downtown hotels with elevators. I bought comic books at outdoor kiosks; we went to movies and ate in restaurants.

In the evenings, Nanny would take me into a bar or cocktail lounge, buy me a chocolate milk, get herself a Tom Collins, and we'd sit and watch television. Every now and then, a program would be in color, which was astonishing. She told me not to tell anyone that we went into bars on our holidays. I knew that if I kept quiet, I'd get more chocolate milk, the cherry from her Tom Collins, might see more TV programs in color, and pocket handfuls of those plastic swizzle sticks. It was a great deal.

Like my brother Ron, with Da, at the bootlegger on Sunday afternoons, I was a willing conspirator. And like her father, Nanny wanted only to get away for a brief time, away from it all. Like him, she needed that drink.

I've lost track of what happened to the liquor cabinet over the years. Someone in the family must have it. The swizzle sticks in the bottom drawer disappeared long before it did. For some reason, though, I feel badly that I don't know where they are. I miss them more than the cabinet.

FROM YELLOW Springs, I drove down 68 to Xenia, then west along 35 into Dayton. It was two-thirty in the afternoon when I got back into the city. I exited onto Patterson south, trundled along the Great Miami River, saw the University of Dayton Arena on the opposite side. Staying with the river, I segued onto Carillon Boulevard, and within seconds was inside Carillon Historical Park.

IN THE park, I saw Dayton history: the Newcom Tavern, a two-story log house with a stone fireplace, preserved from 1796. I stood in front of a 1924 Sun Oil gas station. I scrutinized the 1905 Wright Flyer III airplane, the camera that recorded the milestone initial flight, a drawing table and sewing machine owned by the Wrights. Antique automobiles, a working 1930s print shop, vintage bicycles.

Sitting on a bench, I spread my arms along its wooden back, stared at trees, river, the carillon—the 150-foot granite, steel, and limestone bell tower that stood against the blue Ohio sky—looked around me, realized how pretty it all was.

MY FATHER was not a handsome man. In fact, in many ways he was rather homely. He was about five-seven, thin, balding, wore glasses, and unless he had been drinking, always seemed rather undemonstrative to us. As a kid, watching my mother iron clothes in the kitchen, I once asked her why she had married him. She stopped, looked up, smiled to herself, and said, "Because I love him."

This was a complete revelation to me. Love was what I'd seen on TV and in the movies: beautiful people, romance, kissing, hugging. I saw no connection between daily events in my home and what I'd seen going on between Gregory Peck and Ann Blyth in *The World in His Arms*, which we'd all gone to see at the Capitol Theater on Yonge Street.

Mom had no diamonds, never got a rose. Her wedding ring was a plain silver band that had to be cut off her finger when her hands swelled with arthritis later in her life. Yet it was Dad who pushed for the fiftieth anniversary renewal of vows in 1979 at St. Monica's Church. We stood behind them—Anne, Ron, Judy, Dennis, and myself. Mom's arthritis had her in a wheelchair by then. She seemed to accept it all. But it was Dad, I noticed, who cried. And watching him cry made me cry too.

When she died, less than five years later, in 1984, he was lost.

That was the year I went to Ashland. That was the year I met Jeanne and Adam, the year I started my own family, without knowing it.

I LEFT Carillon Park, sat in a donut shop on Far Hills Avenue, waited for the Delco shift to end.

It was four o'clock. One more hour.

II

AT FIVE o'clock I was parked at the bottom of the entrance driveway where I'd watched his car disappear that morning. I waited about twenty minutes until the JESUSROX Olds drove by me, turned south on Woodman. He was inside it, alone.

I followed.

I'VE THOUGHT back on this a lot. Jeanne was right. It was crazy. Maybe I was crazy.

But I thought maybe my father could help me. Maybe that's why he'd come with me. Why my whole family was with me, inside me.

AT THE corner of Woodman and Dorothy, instead of turning left, heading home, he continued a block farther and drove into Woodlane Plaza. Pulling in behind him, I stayed back, watched as he parked, got out. I watched him go into the Legacy Lounge.

I angled the Honda between two white lines, got out,

looked around. The sun was still hot. I shielded my eyes. Woodman Lanes Bowling, Goodyear Certified Auto Service. Sew-Biz: Bernini Sewing Machines, The Transmission Shop, Carousel Beauty Colleges. Superpetz, the Pet Food Superstore, was the big item in the plaza.

I COULDN'T see inside. It had a wooden front—vertical planks, painted a turquoise blue, including the door. "Top 40 of the '70s, '80s & '90s," a painting of a guitar. "Proper Attire Required." "You Must Be 21." "No Motorcycle Parking on Sidewalk." "Hours: 7 A.M.–2:30 A.M. Sat/Sun: 12 noon–2:30 A.M." Above the door, one of the legs on the N in "Lounge" was broken off.

I stood out front. Inside was Bobby Swiss.

THROUGH THE door, a small alcove, a pay phone, more signs: "Motorcycle Attire Allowed." "Legacy Lounge Reserves the Right to Refuse Service to Anyone!"

I went in. Into the Legacy Lounge.

IT WAS narrow, dimly lit, smoky blue. There was a jukebox in the corner, two billiards tables, three green-shaded, low-hanging lights over each.

A long, rectangular island bar ahead of me, wine-colored stools with backs on them. Red and white plastic pennants strung across the ceiling: "Bud Racing," and "Bud Driven to Win." In recesses at the back, I saw a dartboard and tables. The clock on the wall had a Budweiser face.

I counted seven men at the bar, two waitresses behind it. Nobody paid any attention to me.

He was on a stool, elbows on the mahogany counter. I

watched as a match flared to life in his hand, saw the cigarette tip brighten as he sucked smoke deep into his lungs.

"YOU WANT chicken noodle soup?"

The waitress had one hand on a ladle, the other on the glass lid of the large tureen. The question caught me off guard, coming out of nowhere as it did. I leaned forward on my stool, stared at the offering. "Not right now," I said. "Maybe later."

"What'll you have?"

"Just a beer. A Bud."

A can appeared from a cooler beneath the counter. No glass. I snapped it open, sipped.

I had left one seat between Bobby Swiss and myself. We had breathing space, but I could feel him there. I could feel him. Beside me.

I looked straight ahead.

III

TIFFANY SHADES over the bar, jugs hanging from hooks, glasses suspended upside down in sliding slots. I sat there for another twenty minutes or so, listening, watching.

Not counting the bartenders, eight of us: two groups of three, on opposite sides, at the far end of the bar. Then just us, here, a little beyond the middle.

I heard the chicken noodle soup lady say something that ended with, ". . . our union rep," and the guy she was talking to high-fived her. Raucous laughter. From the other group, I caught the occasional Goddamn, or Fuck You Guys. More laughter.

The condensation trickled in weaving rivulets down the aluminum sides of my Bud, pooling on the counter. I reached over the bar, took a cardboard Samuel Adams coaster from the pile there, placed it under my beer.

I sat there, wondered if Jeanne had gone to the Trail Drive-In with him.

AT LOW volume, the six o'clock news came on the TV high up in the corner, the lead story something to do with the Oklahoma City bombing back in the spring. A still of the gutted Federal Building, then a shot of Timothy McVeigh. I focused on the close-set, frowning eyes, the narrow, pinched mouth on the screen.

"Maniac," said Bobby Swiss.

I turned, looked at him.

"Fuckin' idiot." The smoke drifted from his mouth, nostrils. "My sister was killed there." He swiveled on his stool, spoke to me. "She worked in one of them offices. Social Security Administration. Had a good job. Wasn't hurtin' nobody. I'd hang the bugger myself if I could."

He seemed to be waiting for me to say something. I'd driven hundreds of miles, waited months to talk to him, planned what I'd say, how I'd introduce myself. Suddenly, it all went out the window. I'd been derailed.

"I'm sorry," I said. And I was. For her. Not for him.

"No time for the past, though, right?"

I was quiet.

"Gotta move on."

The past was all around me. I had no idea what he was talking about.

"One good thing came out of it, though." He looked at me. Brown eyes, like his son. Like Adam.

I managed to speak. "What's that?"

"Made me think. I filled out an organ donor card. Keep it in my wallet, right with my driver's license."

He had moved on. The past was over for him.

I couldn't let it go. "Your sister have any children?"

"Two boys."

I waited.

"But they're teenagers." He tipped his jug, filled his glass.

I ran a finger through the cool sweat on the side of my aluminum can.

"They ain't kids. They'll be fine," he said.

I drained my beer. When the chicken soup lady looked in my direction, I held up the empty can. She brought me another.

I ASKED just to see what he'd say. "You from Oklahoma City?"

"Hell, no. I never even been. It was Lorraine, my sister. Married a fella from there. They divorced. She stayed, worked there, raised the boys." He paused, then: "That fuckin' McVeigh."

"Where are the boys now?"

"With their father. That's what I heard, anyway." He looked at me. "I haven't seen you here before, have I?"

I shook my head.

He waited.

I heard myself: "I work for a newspaper in Toronto. Canada."

He looked interested. "What brings you to Dayton?"

I thought about what I'd told the woman on the phone from the 7-Eleven. "Workin' on an article about the area."

"You a writer?"

135

I nodded. I was beginning to amaze myself.

"Goddamn," he said. "Here long?"

I shrugged. "Couple of days. That's about it."

"What you writin' about?"

I thought. Then I said, "Shift work in large factories. People who work them. Like that."

"You come to the right place." He inhaled the last smoke from his cigarette, ground it out in an ashtray, shook another Marlboro loose from the package lying on the counter in front of him.

"Delco?"

He nodded. "Yup. Most who come in here work there." He lit the cigarette, held the smoke deep in his lungs, expelled it in a stream toward the Tiffany shade. "Dayton Engineering Laboratories Company. Owned by G.M."

"What do you do there?"

"Goin' to put me in your article?" He smiled.

I looked down, unsure how deep I should get in. Then: "No. Just askin'."

"We make shocks and struts. I oversee the packaging. Make sure it's okay for shipping." He shrugged. "It's a livin'."

I heard my father's voice, me asking him if he liked his job at the *Star*. *It's a living*. I heard my own answer to myself, when no one had even asked the question, just as I hadn't asked Bobby Swiss—realized that it was one of the things men would confess to, unbidden, one of the bonds so many of us shared, and was stunned.

"YOU FROM Dayton?" I wanted to hear what he'd say.

"Kentucky. Ashland. It's on the Ohio River, near West

Virginia. 'Bout a hundred miles from here. Been in Dayton twenty years though."

"Why Dayton?"

"Dayton, Cincinnati, Columbus, Akron. Could've been any of 'em." He smiled. "You know that car, the Pontiac GTO?"

"I know of it."

"In Kentucky, they say GTO stands for Goin' To Ohio. It's where there's work. Can get a good union job. You know of Ashland?"

"Not much."

"If you aren't at Ashland Oil, jobs are scarce."

I was in real deep now, in territory I'd never even dreamed of entering. None of it was planned. It was just happening.

"The Judds are from Ashland." Then he chuckled. "There's a Judd Plaza. Chuck Woolery, the game-show host. They even got a street named after him—Chuck Woolery Boulevard."

"Lots of celebrities."

"Lots? Right. Sure. Oh, I forgot." He gestured with his hand, expansively. "George Reeves."

George Reeves. I actually knew the name. It was from my generation. "Superman?" It struck a nerve, one that the other names hadn't tweaked. I was suddenly back on the floor at Maxwell Avenue, 1953, in front of the black-and-white RCA. Wednesday nights, 7 P.M. WBEN-TV, channel 4, Buffalo. The never-ending battle for truth, justice, and the American Way. Brought to you by Kellogg's. "He's from Ashland?"

"Well, not exactly. He was born in Iowa, they say. His mother's parents lived in Ashland. When his own parents broke up, his mother moved back to Ashland for a while. He did some growin' up there."

I tilted my head.

"He's a celebrity. We'll take what we can get. You remember watchin' him?"

"It was my favorite show." It was true.

"Killed himself."

"So they say. As I recall, it was never clear."

"I was just a little kid."

"I'm a bit older than you." I looked at him. "It was 1959."

He raised his eyebrows. "Pretty good memory."

I nodded. "I'm good at the past," I said.

"WHAT DO you think of that?" Bobby Swiss nodded toward the television above us.

I glanced up. Some kind of triangular, glass, architectural wonder was on the screen, at water's edge.

"Rock and Roll Hall of Fame. Cleveland. Opens in about a month. Big news there. Big tourist attraction. Architect is the same guy who built the addition onto the Louvre in Paris."

My eyebrows rose upward. A modern-day pyramid, on Lake Erie.

A list of the 1995 inductees appeared, superimposed on the building's image: The Allman Brothers, Al Green, Janis Joplin, Led Zeppelin, Martha and the Vandellas, Neil Young, Frank Zappa.

"What the fuck," he said.

I was quiet.

"I couldn't even name a song that any of them cut. How about you?"

"Maybe Neil Young. Canadian, I think. Maybe Martha and the Vandellas. 'Dancin' in the Street.' "

"Del Shannon," he said. "Where the fuck is Del Shannon? How come he's not in there?" He looked at me.

"I dunno," I said. And I didn't.

"Old Del shot himself."

I nodded, thoughtfully.

"You gotta go way back. Gotta go to the roots. Chuck Berry, Sam Cooke, Fats Domino, Buddy Holly. And the King. Elvis."

"You're probably right."

"The Coasters, Clyde McPhatter, Roy Orbison, Otis Redding, The Platters."

"You sound like you know this stuff."

"Love it."

"I thought you weren't big on the past."

He looked at me with wonder. "Hell, music ain't the past. Music is forever. I can put my tapes on in my car right now, and it's there. There's a song, 'American Pie,' about 'The Day the Music Died.' The music never died. It was those assholes ridin' around in cars or on motorcycles or in airplanes or doin' drugs that got killed. Not their music."

JESUSROX, I thought. "Whatever happened to Del Shannon?" I remembered "Runaway," "Hats Off to Larry."

"Shot himself. Age fifty-one. All the good ones, the music killed them. It consumed them. They gave themselves to it, now they're gone. But not their music. No, sir. Not their music. The music is forever."

An image of Graceland Wedding Chapel, Las Vegas, rose up in the back of my head. "Even Elvis—" I started.

"—is dead. Age forty-two. Buddy Holly, Ritchie Valens, the Big Bopper, Otis Redding, even Rick Nelson—

139

plane crashes, all of them. Clyde McPhatter, heart attack, age forty. Roy Orbison, heart attack, age fifty-two. Mama Cass, heart attack. Sam Cooke, Marvin Gaye, even John Lennon, shot to death. And I haven't even started on the drug overdoses. Morrison, Joplin, Hendrix . . ."

But part of me had stopped listening. I was thinking about Jeanne's line, about loving singers who had died violently in motorized vehicles.

I was quiet. I'd heard a lot of this before.

AFTER A third beer, I had no plan left. Finally, when he'd drained his jug, finished the fifth cigarette, he sat back. "Gotta go," he said.

I half smiled and nodded.

"Wife'll have dinner ready."

I'd wondered. Now I knew. But I wanted more. "Got kids?"

"One," he said. "Got a boy. Sixteen." He frowned, added no more. Then, "You here for a couple of days, you say?"

"That's right."

"Might see you tomorrow. I'm here most days after work."

I studied the strong chin, the slicked-back hair, the five o'clock shadow that Adam favored. I wanted to ask him if he'd ever gone to the Trail Drive-In, to Crisp's, to the Bluegrass for a hot dog and a root beer or the Flying Saucer Burger with the special sauce.

But I didn't. I couldn't. That had been more than twenty years ago.

I looked around, up at the TV, thought of Nanny, the bars in Buffalo. I took a plastic swizzle stick, put it in my pocket, left.

Thirteen

I

I WENT back to the Hampton Inn, rested for an hour, went for dinner at a Pizza Hut nearby. When I got back, I phoned Jeanne. It was our shortest conversation since I'd left. I didn't know how to tell her anything, and she didn't ask. With grace, without details, we enjoyed the contact. It was enough. I was tired. I was more than tired. I was drained.

"YOU CAN live too long," my father had said to me, in one of the sporadic retrievals of his old self, on his ninetieth birthday, four months before he died.

For a moment, he knew what was happening to him, how he was losing his dignity.

Then just as unexpectedly, he was gone. "Call the Musicians' Union," he said.

I was quiet.

"Make sure my dues are paid up."

I ALREADY mentioned finding the little brush that he had used to clean his electric razor. I also found his folding nail file just last month—the one I borrowed one day several years ago—while looking for the TV remote control down the sides of our bed. And it was Jeanne who found his scapular medal on the floor under his bed while moving it aside for vacuuming. A stylized cross on a chain, he had worn the medal around his neck all his life, even though he was anything but a devout Catholic. Nevertheless, he wasn't anything else. He knew what he was supposed to be, even if he couldn't be it.

Pieces of him dotted our house, like shells washed up on the shore.

IN HIS wallet he kept his TTC—Toronto Transit Commission—Blind Pass, his social insurance card, birth certificate, his Old Age Security card, an Ontario Senior Citizens' Privilege Card, one of Dennis's business cards, his Toronto Star Limited Employee Photo ID Card, dated November 24, 1964. He had no bank card, no credit cards. He said he couldn't see well enough to use them.

In the top drawer of his dresser, after he died, in a plastic case, I found a small metal plaque with his name engraved on it. It stated that he was a Life Member of the Toronto Musicians Association, Local 149 A.F. of M. "THIS TOKEN WAS PRESENTED TO *Thomas Nolan* IN RECOGNITION OF TWENTY-FIVE YEARS CONTINUOUS MEMBERSHIP."

His dues were paid up.

THAT NIGHT, in the Hampton Inn, he appeared again. But it wasn't just a dream. It was more.

Things were changing.

WE ARE in a recording studio somewhere, surrounded by microphones, tape machines, a small orchestra. My father turns and points to my sisters, to Anne and Judy, who are here with us. They left me here, he says.

I don't know what he means.

Then he comes over to me and says I'm not leaving until I get some satisfaction.

I look at the orchestra, at my sisters. The musicians are packing away their instruments. They didn't leave you here, I say. We found you here. You got here by yourself.

Dennis comes in with my brother, Ron. They hold him by the shoulders and try to calm him down. I know what's going on, he says to them. I know exactly what's going on. Then Ron takes a small, smooth stone from his pocket, and puts it in his father's hand. Tommy Nolan closes his hand over it, relaxes visibly.

He looks at me. Don't be a fool, he says.

I don't want to be a fool. I stare at his clenched fist, see the knuckles white, know he is holding the stone. Ron smiles, puts his arm around Dad's shoulder. Then my older brother speaks to me. It's okay, he says. Everything's okay. He's coming with me. I'll calm him down.

Dennis, Anne and Judy, and I tell the remaining musicians they might as well go home. The recording session is over. We help them carry their instruments out to a parking lot, put them in car trunks, backseats. My eye is drawn to the brass gleam of a trombone resting in the plush purple velvet lining of its case.

It begins to rain.

WHEN I woke up, I was drenched in sweat, alone. It was 4 A.M. I got up, went to the bathroom, dried myself with a towel, had a drink of water, got back into bed with the light on, sat there. My night sweats, I was thinking. They're not gone.

That was when it happened.

The noise was like a gunshot. Without warning, the wooden coffee table in front of the love seat split down the middle. I got up, went over, looked down at it, stunned.

Solid wood, split in half, a sound like a thunderclap.

I stared at it, touched it, sat back on the edge of the bed, dizzy.

I PUT on the coffeemaker. I didn't sleep anymore that night.

IN THE morning, at the desk, the lady looked skeptical when I told her.

I shrugged. I didn't blame her.

"Maybe it was a contraction of heat and cold. Maybe it had something to do with the room being dry—you know, no humidity."

I was still getting that look.

"Just bill me for it."

"I don't even know how much it will be."

"I'm sure you can find out. You've got my credit card imprint. I accept responsibility. It can't be that much."

While I was talking to her, I put my hand in my pocket. My fingers galvanized at the touch of a small, smooth stone there. Slowly, catching my breath, I closed my hand around it, squeezed it.

II

MY FATHER'S tackle box.

He loved to fish. Mom told me once that he took it up

back in the 1930s, because my brother Ron, only a little kid then, had an operation on his mastoid—the bone behind the ear—and couldn't go swimming, couldn't get water in his ear as a result. Mastoiditis, I think it was called. Ron loved to swim, and was good at it.

Dad wanted to find something he could do with him, something they could do together, that might help a kid forget that he was drydocked for the summer.

Tommy Nolan, in his thirties, worked for *The Globe & Mail* back then, and the newspaper owned The Globe Park in Port Dover, on Lake Erie, about eighty miles southwest of Toronto. The park consisted of a dozen or so small cottages that the paper made available to employees and their families as part of their annual two-week summer vacation, if they wished to avail themselves of them. It was a part of my childhood too for a while: the clay in the cliffs, corn roasts on the beach at night, the sandbars, perch fishing. The outhouses with two holes, side by side, fascinated me. It all ended in 1952, when Dad left *The Globe* and went to work for the *Star*.

For the first time in more than twenty years, he had to find someplace new to go for his annual two weeks vacation, so we headed for Bancroft, Ontario, 160 miles northeast of the city. Bancroft was a small town in the Kawartha Lakes district, on the Canadian Shield, famous for its annual Gemboree, which attracted rock hounds from all over to savor its mineral deposits. It was also surrounded by beautiful, clear lakes, wonderful fishing.

Dad's sister, Eleanor, my aunt, had moved there when her husband, Tommy Weatherell, a car mechanic, had wanted to open his own service station. They also built the Homestead Restaurant beside their gas station and their bungalow on Highway 28, and Eleanor ran it. Several lodges or cottage group owners in the area that didn't serve meals would refer their guests there. Eleanor was Mom's friend from her schoolgirl days. In fact, she had met Dad through Eleanor.

For several years in the fifties, every summer, we rented a two-room cabin with a rowboat, on Bow Lake. It was one of five cabins that were operated under the name Ida-Ho Lodge by the middle-aged couple that lived at the end of the road—Jack and Ida Horsepool. Ours had double bunks in the bedroom: Mom and Dad on the bottom, Dennis and I on the top. The other room was mostly a kitchen. There was an outhouse—no indoor plumbing. Mom washed the dishes by carrying water up from the lake. There was no refrigerator, just an icebox. We drove down the highway daily to Paudash Lake, watched a man with giant tongs climb into the sawdust-filled icehouse and pull up a chunk that had been cut from the lake and stored since the winter, then loaded it onto newspaper in the trunk of our car.

Every evening, right after dinner, my father would take us out in the rowboat and we'd fish for smallmouth bass until it got dark. Hula popper, crazy crawler, jitterbug. The memory of the splash of a smallmouth hitting a surface lure on those calm July evenings—the rod bending, the water like glass, our collars turned up against the fall of night—can still make my heart race.

Mom stayed behind in the cabin and read a book. It was her time alone. But she waited for us. We could see it in her eyes when we came through the door, closing it quickly to keep the mosquitoes out.

Eleanor died of cancer in 1966, age fifty-five. Her husband, Tommy Weatherell, eventually remarried and moved away. He outlived her by twenty-one years, dying in 1987.

My father's tackle box. Behind the furnace in my basement.

THAT SAME day last summer that Jeanne and I detoured down the Bird's Creek turnoff in search of the vanished Bancroft Drive-In, I also stopped on the highway at Bow Lake and turned onto the private dirt road that had once led to those cabins. There is no wooden sign for Ida-Ho Lodge anymore. The cabins have been torn down. I stared at the ground where they had been. You'd never know they had ever existed. Like the drive-in: disappeared—not a trace. Jack and Ida Horsepool's names are no longer on their mailbox. New people live in that house at the foot of the road.

Driving from Bow Lake into Bancroft, I saw that the Sunoco service station was now Wayne's World, a business that sold snowmobiles. Someone had converted The Homestead Restaurant into a private home.

LAS VEGAS, the Poconos, drive-in theaters in New York State. The next summer, in July, it was time to try something different. Jeanne and I rented a cottage on Paudash Lake for one week, the site of the long-gone sawdust-filled icehouse, a few miles down the highway from my boyhood.

I keep going back to my childhood. I know it wasn't perfect, but it doesn't matter. I hear the irrational siren songs that are my past, balance them against the longing for a better future.

TWO BEDROOMS, a living-dining-kitchen area with a cathedral ceiling, an all-glass front with sliding doors leading onto a cedar deck that hovered over the water's edge. Stone fireplace, TV, VCR, microwave, telephone, gas barbecue, a sixteen-foot aluminum boat with a 30 hp Yamaha, all nestled in pines, tall hemlocks, and birches, with three hundred feet of lake frontage for complete privacy. Like nothing I'd ever seen before. Certainly not on Bow Lake.

It even had indoor plumbing. A shower no less.

Cold beer, smoked salmon with onions and capers, bread, cheese, sipping Caesars on the deck, the sun on Jeanne's skin. Skinny-dipping at night, the moon on the water, the shower of northern Ontario stars across the sky. Mist rising off the lake at dawn, the loon's call, an otherworldly echo. Lovemaking, indoors and out.

On the second morning there, I rose at 5 A.M., took my fishing rod and tackle box, went out alone. Anchored in a secluded bay, the world heart-stoppingly peaceful, I thought of my father, how he would have loved it, and I missed him. It's funny—I don't usually miss him. I remember him, but missing him is for some reason rare. This was one of those rare times. I pictured him with his hat on, the hand-rolled cigarette dangling from his mouth.

The water was so clear and still, I could see the bottom, a dozen feet down: rocks, logs, a sudden drop-off. Beneath the surface. I had only to see beneath the surface.

Memories, like sawdust-covered ice, slow to melt.

It was the outdoor lovemaking that flourished, though. The beauty, the privacy, the freedom. Jeanne and I did it as often as we felt like it. It was wonderful. Sun, moon, water, and the earth itself—they were all sexual. I understood the primal drive of the ancient farmer and wife who copulated in the fields on a spring night to nudge the gods toward a full harvest.

JEANNE AND I had three glorious days alone together. On the fourth morning, Adam took the bus up from Toronto and we met him in Bancroft. He had two days off that week from his summer job at Mr. Lube.

His visit added a new dimension to our holiday. He completed it. We had been happy when we were alone. We were happy when he was with us. We were happy driving him back to meet the bus two days later, anticipating our last two days together alone.

We were a family. We grilled chicken breasts on the barbecue, ate hot dogs, read magazines, floated on rubber rafts, hands and feet trailing in the water, lay on the dock at night and watched shooting stars, roasted marshmallows in the rock-ringed fire pit outside.

After dinner, both nights, Adam and I went fishing. We took the boat down the lake, among the stumps and lily pads, where the water was still and not too deep, cut the engine and drifted. Hula popper, crazy crawler, jitterbug.

Jeanne stayed behind in the cottage and read. She waited for us. We could see it in her eyes when we came through the door.

ON THE Sunday, our final evening alone, we drove down the Lower Faraday Road to Coe Hill and dined out at Winnifred's. We had a bottle of wine with dinner. The waitress lit the candle on our table.

On the way back to the cottage, we saw a deer, watched it saunter off into the woods as we drove by.

LIKE THAT ancient farmer and his wife, we hoped for a harvest. Hoped and waited.

In August, when nothing happened, again, we began to wonder.

III

THAT AFTERNOON in Dayton, I stopped at the Root Beer Stand on Woodman Drive, not far from Delco. With my root beer, I had a foot-long coney, and knew that I was going back to the Legacy Lounge, one more time.

Fourteen

I

Do I have regrets? Many. Every day, I regret that my mother died alone in a hospital and that I was not there. I regret that my father's mind went before his body did, that he died alone in a hospital and that I was not there.

I regret a thousand harsh words, misunderstandings, bad decisions, impatiences.

Regret is not what I feel when I remember that my son, at birth, did not live. There are no words for what I feel. None.

I remember sitting on the floor in the room we had set aside for a nursery, disassembling the crib we had purchased, sealing the screws, nuts, bolts in an envelope.

DAD TOLD me he used to bicycle up to Leaside from Cabbagetown, five miles maybe, to the airfield there, during World War One, to see an airplane up close. He told me he used to swim in the Don River, now called the Dirty Don. He told me he cut his foot in Riverdale Park on a broken bottle when he was a kid, and the infection was so serious that he almost lost his foot.

I remember him taking me to a movie once, just him and me. He held my hand on the street. It was 1954. We went to see *Twenty Thousand Leagues Under the Sea* at the Imperial Theater on Yonge Street. He told me that he had read the book as a kid, and wanted to see the movie.

I remember in the 1950s when Mom used to iron clothes in the kitchen, she always hummed a distinctive tune. I asked her what it was.

"When It's Springtime in the Rockies," she said.

Why do you hum it? I asked.

Because it's my favorite.

Why is it your favorite?

The silence preceding a truth. Then: When I was a little girl I saw a picture of Lake Louise and thought it was the most beautiful place I'd ever seen. I thought I'd like to go there someday.

These are some of the things they told me.

These were my parents: before I was born, holding my hand on Yonge Street, ironing clothes in the kitchen, humming.

II

"YOU WANT chicken noodle soup?" she asked.

"I think I do." I sat on the stool, rested my elbows on the mahogany counter, left one seat empty between Bobby Swiss and myself.

She ladled it out, set a steaming bowl in front of me.

"It's good." He smiled at me through a haze of blue smoke, Marlboro dangling from his fingers.

"And a Bud," I added.

She set the can in front of me, drifted up the bar.

"I'd have some," he said, "but it might spoil my dinner. Wife'd be mad. This"—he tapped his beer glass with

the fingers holding the cigarette—"don't spoil nothin'."
The ash fell off his cigarette. He brushed it down the
counter.

I sipped the soup. He was right. It was good.

"You get any of your writin' done?"

I thought about it. "A bit."

He shook his head. "Goddamn," he said.

I smiled.

"I guess you use a computer."

"It's the only way."

"Goddamn." He sat back. "I can't imagine writin'
nothin'." He was looking at me with one eyebrow up, the
other down. "Matter of fact, I can't even imagine readin'
nothin'." He laughed.

I thought of Adam, his son, a student of English literature.

"Wife used to read too much. Whenever I caught her,
I told her she was wastin' her time. She liked them pocket
books, them romances. Found out that she was readin' in
the bathroom, just so's I wouldn't complain. After that, I
left her alone about it."

I nodded as though I understood. But I didn't. Not at
all. "You have to pick your battles," I said. "They have to
be ones worth fighting."

"Exactly." He sipped his beer.

I finished my soup, pushed the bowl aside.

"WHAT YOU seen of Dayton?"

"Not as much as I'd like. It looks like a pretty city."

"It's a city," he said. "Like most others."

"Carillon Park."

He nodded.

"Lots of Wright brothers stuff."

"Lots of Wright brothers," he agreed. "Wright-Patterson Air Force Base."

"John Glenn. His name pops up too."

He smiled. "John Glenn Parkway. Like Chuck Woolery Boulevard. Not much difference, as I see it."

"One was an astronaut. A senator. The other hosted *The Dating Game*."

"Like I said. Not much difference." He drained his glass, refilled it from his jug.

THE NEWS came on the TV. More about Oklahoma City. I waited to see if he'd react.

Instead: "Shoot some pool?" He took the cigarette from his mouth after he'd asked the question.

"I'm not much good at it."

"Don't matter. It's a buck a game. Loser pays. One of the few things I can afford."

The Federal Building, photos before and after, commentary too low to hear. He looked away. Not interested in the past, I thought.

I turned and stared at the two tables, the green velvet, the low-hanging lights. It'd been a long time. I thought of Uncle Jim and me, shooting pool that time in the Legion Hall. "Why not?"

"IS THAT your license plate out front?"

He chalked his cue. "JESUSROX?"

"Yeah."

"What made you think it was mine?"

"You seemed to know your music, when we were talking yesterday."

He angled the cue against the table, set the cigarette in an ashtray, freed both hands, ran his fingers through his hair a couple of times, pulled it from the back of his collar. "It's mine all right. One of them vanity plates. Wife give it to me as a birthday present two years ago. She knows about me and rock music. The Jesus part, though, that was her idea."

"You not religious?"

"Nah." He picked up his cue, leaned down, sighted along it and the white ball. "Kind of has a nice ring to it, though. Jesus wasn't a bad guy. Didn't hurt nobody. He helped them prostitutes, didn't he? Mary Magdalene? My kind of guy."

That clack sound, after the stroke, so clean and sharp and pure.

"What's your wife do?" I asked.

He straightened, picked up his cigarette. "Watches TV." He smiled, looked at me. "Lots of things. Used to, anyway. Now she stays home." He picked up his beer from the cardboard coaster on the table's edge, held it without drinking. "My son," he said. "He's a full-time job." His brow furrowed.

"Sixteen. Isn't that what you told me yesterday?"

"Yup."

"Teenager. Sixteen-year-old can be a full-time job."

"It's more'n that."

He stepped aside so that I could take my shot. I bent toward it.

"He's schizophrenic."

I didn't take the shot. I straightened.

He shrugged. The tip of his cigarette glowed fiercely as he pulled the smoke deep, held it, expelled it at the ceiling.

"I DON'T know much about that," I said.

"You learn fast."

155

"I'm sure you do."

"Lot of that Jesus stuff started to show up in our house after Donny was diagnosed. The wife, you know."

I didn't say anything.

"He was always a strange kid. Marks were all over the place in school, up, down. You'd never know. Then he hit puberty. Became a teenager. Acted crazier than ever. Started talkin' crazy, ramblin' all over the place. Teachers didn't know what to make of him. Told me a story once about how he was hallucinatin' about a Black & Decker drill. I didn't know what the hell he was talkin' about."

I took my shot, stood back, watched the balls roll, settle.

"If you were to phone my house right now, and he answered, he'd say 'Stand by one,' or somethin' nuts like that. He repeats stuff he hears on TV. Sometimes he sounds like a paid advertisement." He put the Marlboro to his lips, inhaled, set it again in the ashtray on the table's rim. He chalked his cue. "Every now and then, he's fine, like he knows somethin's wrong with him."

My father, in his last days.

"He's not a bad kid. Wouldn't hurt a fly. You can't leave him alone though. Might burn the house down."

"He's on medication?"

"Lots. Three of these, two of those. Blues, reds. Pammy—that's the missus—she takes care of all that. Me, I go to work, to Delco, package up the fuckin' shocks and struts, make sure we can pay for the blues, the reds, whatever other color of pill he's takin'. It's a livin'."

"I'm sorry."

"Don't be. He's a good kid. Ain't his fault. Doctors explained it to me. His wiring's all fucked up. Needs his chemistry balanced."

"We all need our chemistry balanced."

He looked at me. "Ain't it the truth." He took his shot. That clack, so pure and sweet. Balls jumped across the velvet, silent.

I RECOGNIZED the glass pyramid. Another ad for the Rock and Roll Hall of Fame appeared on the TV. *Opening September 2, 1995.*

He looked up at it.

"Why Cleveland?" I asked.

"Lobbyin'. More'n six hundred thousand people signed a petition." He squinted, thinking. "Cleveland can make a claim," he said. "Know who Alan Freed was?"

"Deejay? Is that the guy?"

"That's him." He smiled, impressed. "Pioneered rock and roll. Probably named it. He's Cleveland."

I nodded.

He leaned to sight his shot. "Chuck Berry made his first public appearance there. Elvis played his first concert north of the Mason-Dixon line in Cleveland." He settled the cue softly between thumb and forefinger. "Joe Walsh, Phil Ochs, the Raspberries, Wild Cherry, Bobby Womack—all Cleveland." Hair fell across his forehead.

It was my turn to be impressed.

The clack.

The cue ball settled, a faint blue chalk mark on its perfect white surface.

"DID YOU know Roy Orbison died the year after he got into the Hall? He was the first to die after being inducted."

I shook my head. "Didn't know that."

"Fact. Inducted in '87, at the second annual dinner, Waldorf-Astoria, New York. Dead in '88.

157

" 'Only the Lonely,' " I said.

" 'Running Scared.' " He sighed. " 'Crying.' God-damn. He could hit that high note." He looked at me. "You know he died of a broken heart."

I didn't say anything.

"He wrote 'Only the Lonely' in his car, 'cause there wasn't enough room in the house. His first wife died in a motorcycle accident. Two of their three sons were killed when his house went up in flames two years later. He turned to prostitutes. Used to go down to a cat house in Juarez."

I didn't ask how he knew all this. I never doubted him. I hadn't asked how he knew about Mary Magdalene either. You never know what somebody knows.

"You can hear his broken heart when he sings." He looked at me. "But the music," he said, "it ain't dead. I can put it on in my car."

"NAME'S BOBBY." He held his hand out.

"Leo." I took his hand, squeezed it.

"You married? Got kids?"

"Married. Got a son. He's twenty-one."

"He workin'? Or still in school?"

"School. University."

"What's he studyin'?"

"English literature."

He whistled. "Books. Readin'. Writin'." He shook his head. "And you're a writer. Chip off the old block. Takes after the old man." He ran his hands through the hair on the sides of his head, pulled it loose from his collar at the back. "Donny—my boy—he likes maps. Studies 'em. Marks 'em up with a yellow highlighter, makes notes.

Sometimes I think he's tryin' to figure out where he is, where he should go, like he's lost. You know?"

I nodded, thought for a moment. "I think I know." I reached into my back pocket, took out the pocket guide to Dayton I'd been carrying around, looked at it. "Here." I held it out.

He looked at it, at me.

"I've been using it to get around the city. It's full of maps. I don't need it anymore. Give it to Donny."

He took it, was quiet. He turned it over. Then he put it in his own back pocket. "Thanks."

"It's nothing."

"He'll love it."

"My pleasure." I finished my Bud, put the can down on the table's rim.

He was quiet again. He was still thinking about it. I could tell. I picked up the cue ball, closed my hand on the hard, white, round surface, squeezing. Like a stone. Perfect.

"I CAN hear the dinner bell ringin'."

We snapped the cues into the wall rack, stood back.

"Will I see you again?"

"I doubt it. Heading back tomorrow." I didn't know what to say, so I asked a question. "Besides the chicken noodle soup, what's good to eat around here? Where's a good spot for dinner?"

"You like Italian?"

"I like nearly every kind of food."

"Try Mamma DiSalvo's. Go down to Stroop, just south of here, make a right. Few blocks along. Near Marshall, on the north side. Tell her Bobby Swiss sent you."

159

"I just might do that."

He clucked his tongue. "And stop in Cleveland. Have a look at the Hall of Fame. Eighth fuckin' wonder of the world. Think of the music that's in there."

"I just might do that too." We shook hands. I was touching him. Again. It didn't hurt a bit. It was okay.

"It's in the music," he said. He smiled. "You'll hear old Roy cryin', if you listen hard."

"Take care." I squeezed his hand, touched his arm, and left.

Outside, I stared at the Olds. JESUSROX.

You can hear everybody crying, I thought, if you listen hard.

AT MAMMA DiSalvo's, I told her Bobby Swiss had sent me. She gave me a nice table in the back and I ordered the ravioli and a half liter of red. It was terrific.

WHEN I phoned home that night, Jeanne told me that she was cleaning the house.

"Must be spick and span by now," I said.

"My heart beats a little faster every time I find a new little dust pile. You've no idea."

"You're right. I have no idea."

"The dishes are stackin' up for you."

"Leave 'em. I'm coming home. Leaving in the morning."

There was silence on the other end of the phone.

"Right after the continental breakfast."

I'm not sure, I could be wrong, but I thought I could hear her crying too. When I asked her, she said no, but I think she was.

III

MY FATHER liked big band music, had played banjo, guitar, trombone. He thought Bernstein's score for *West Side Story* was terrific. He was a Lifetime Member of the Musicians' Union, Local 149, A.F. of M.

My mother liked humming "When It's Springtime in the Rockies" while she ironed in the kitchen.

Maybe Bobby Swiss was right. Maybe it was all in the music, if you just listened.

THAT NIGHT, I slept rather peacefully. Around 4 A.M., though, I did hear the bathroom door—the only door in the room—open and close once, by itself. It could have been the air-conditioning coming on and going off, creating a vacuum, changing air pressure in the room. I don't know.

The next morning, the stone that I was sure I had left in my pocket was sitting on top of the TV. I picked it up, held it, felt its smooth, round surface.

III

The Salmon and the Eel

Every time you pray . . .
you will understand
that prayer is an education.

—FYODOR DOSTOEVSKY
The Brothers Karamazov

Fifteen

I

AFTER YOGURT, muffin, orange juice, and coffee the next morning, I left the Hampton Inn, got onto 70, and headed east out of Dayton, away from the city where Orville and Wilbur gave birth to the idea for flight, took it to Kitty Hawk, changed everything. The place where they went home to be buried. I left Delco, the Legacy Lounge, the bungalow on Galewood, doors that opened and closed in the night.

The sun was in my eyes. I pulled the visor down. I wasn't going back the way I came.

AT ROUTE 42, I went north, bypassing Columbus. When I hit Delaware, I saw the signs for Ohio Wesleyan University, turned east on 36, got onto I-71. I had one more stop to make, up on Lake Erie. Even if it wasn't open yet, I wanted to see it.

PLACE NAMES recurred, in sets, in groups: Dixie, Bowling Green, the Ottawa River, St. Clair. More Main Streets than there had been swizzle sticks in the liquor cabinet on Maxwell Avenue. Past Mansfield, I saw another sign, another example. Like Bowling Green, like Dixie, Ashland had namesakes. Ohio had an Ashland too. It was late afternoon, I needed to eat, rest, so I went west the few miles along 96, out of curiosity.

I HAD a chicken salad sandwich and coffee in the Food Court of the John C. Myers Convocation Center, at Ashland University—another deeply rooted sapling in the forest of higher learning spread so generously across Ohio.

They gave me honey for the coffee instead of sugar.

I read *The Collegian*, the newspaper published weekly by the journalism department, pretended I was a writer, like I had told Bobby Swiss. Surrounded by a hundred landscaped acres, young people opening doors on their futures, I dreamed Adam was the student editor. I saw everyone in my family living different lives, in different places. Anything was possible.

I broke open the packet of honey, squeezed it into my coffee, stirred it in.

THINGS HAVE a momentum, an inevitability. When Fran and I broke up, back in 1972, I think I was in shock. I still don't know exactly how it happened. It was a snowball rolling downhill, gathering bulk, unmanageable.

Afterward, the wound closed over, scarred, hardened. But when the weather is damp, when I turn my neck a certain way, I can feel that memory, the past, like shrapnel, shift, sit heavily, throb, then mercifully, fade away once more.

I haven't seen Fran in twenty-three years. I heard she moved to Los Angeles, was working in real estate. I don't know. That's what I heard.

Aidan, my stillborn son, is buried in an unmarked grave, in an area known as Child Common Ground beneath a giant oak in Mount Pleasant Cemetery. He is in plot 391, section 42. You can see the spot when you're driving along Moore. It's just opposite Lumley Avenue.

I remember a friend telling me at the time that there was a certain cushion of mercy in the fact that I never got to know him. What that person didn't understand was that I did get to know him. You live in your imagination. I knew him. I knew him well.

WHEN JEANNE still hadn't gotten pregnant, after all our adventures, after temperature taking and charts, we were more than a little puzzled. After all, we had both proven fertile in the past: Adam. Aidan.

We took it to the next level. We agreed to visit Siliaris, our family doctor, see what he had to say.

Jeanne volunteered to go first. Bloodwork suggested that she was ovulating. A month or two later, back to the lab, more tests. This time it was a series of intravaginal ultrasounds. Again, everything seemed okay.

Then it was my turn. Where Jeanne had agreed to the usual feminine probing, I had to agree, in male fashion, to be rather more active. I was given a small, sealed container, plastic, instructed to go home and supply a semen sample at my leisure, then deliver it within the hour to the medical laboratory at Danforth and Coxwell.

Into the plastic jar. It was a first. Definitely a first.

What the hell. Jeanne and I turned it into a kind of game. With the exception of the small embarrassment of handing it over to the receptionist while she asked for the appropriate information, it turned out not to be so bad after all.

—✺—

"IT SAYS here that your sperm count is low. Around four-teen million. Motility's a little low too." Siliaris was Greek, about my age. He had a remarkable, flowing, dark mus-tache, glasses. He nudged the specs up his nose a little as he read the printout.

I didn't know what to say. Fourteen million sounded like a hell of a lot to me.

"I'm going to refer you to a urologist. He's also a fer-tility expert. Samuelson. Out in the west end. I'll have Donna set it up for you."

"Okay." A pause. I was confused. Then: "I've told you about the baby in the past. What was that—some kind of a fluke?"

"Not at all. That was a long time ago." He paused. "You're older now. Things have changed." He was still studying the paper in his hands. "I'm not real good at reading these charts. Not my speciality. But something here suggests to me that there might be a specific cause. Nothing serious. That's why I'd like you to see Samuelson. This is his area. He does it all day long. Find out what he has to say." He looked at me. "He'll know."

I sat quiet, humbled a bit. I'd never suspected. Some-thing was amiss. Finally: "Okay," I said. "Let's do it."

Driving home, staring into the traffic, I heard the words again. The past few years, Jeanne and I, all our attempts, began, slowly, to slide into place. *You're older now. Things have changed.*

SAMUELSON WAS in his sixties, a jovial fellow who under-stood the personal nature of his business and took pains to put people at ease. He had indeed been doing it all day long, for years.

He looked up from the chart, over his wire-rimmed eyeglasses, stared at me, smiled. "You've got an infection."

I just stared back at him, silent.

"Here," he said, placing the paper on the desk between us, turning it so I could read. "This number." He pointed with his finger. "The white blood cell count is too high. It's indicative of an infection."

I looked at it, sat back.

"I want to check for myself, though."

"How?"

"In here."

We went into another room.

"I'm going to check your prostate."

I groaned.

He chuckled. "I know."

It was nothing new. I was moving into that area where it was an annual event for men my age. But it wasn't exactly my favorite.

"I'll be quick."

And he was. Without telling me he was going to, he pressed suddenly on my prostate gland, exerting momentary pressure—discomfort rather than pain—then held a small glass slide at the end of my penis. I was shocked to find myself exuding a bit of liquid onto the slide.

"Jesus," I said, stunned. "What the hell happened there?"

"Prostatic fluid," he said. "I can find out what I want to know in a minute." He left me, went over to the microscope in the corner, placed the slide beneath the lens, peered down the scope, adjusting for clarity. Without looking up, he said, "You can get dressed."

I slid off the table, tucked my shirt in, buckled up.

"You'll be a bit uncomfortable for a few hours. It'll fade."

"Good."

His chuckle was comforting. "Can you imagine how many times a day I do that?"

I shook my head. "I have to admit, I can't."

"You've got prostatitis, Mr. Nolan."

I was seated on the opposite side of his desk, back in the first room. It didn't sound good. "I don't know what that is."

"Inflammation of the prostate. Infection. Probably chronic bacterial prostatitis."

I looked at him. "You have my full attention."

"You probably got it from a bladder infection. The bacteria can get into the prostate from backward flow. It's not transmittable from one person to another. Your partner didn't give it to you, and you can't give it to her, so there's no reason for concern there. It's self-contained."

"How serious is it? What should I do?"

"I'm going to put you on antibiotics. Six weeks to start. I'll see you again in six weeks, and you can bring your own semen sample next time." He smiled. "Easier that way." He pulled over his prescription pad, began scribbling. "The infection, you see, causes the white blood cells to increase, and the sperm can't get out properly. It's like they're being blocked, and they bounce around inside you. That's why your count is low. The antibiotics should lower the white cell count, if not get rid of all of them. That way, things should pick up." He finished writing, looked at me. "You came in here with what you thought was a fertility problem, and it is. But what you've got is a larger, general health problem. It's a good thing you're here." The smile again, a kind one.

"How common is this?"

"Much more common than you'd think. It's not easily diagnosed, as you've just found out. You know," he said, thoughtfully, candidly, "you've been sick for a long time."

I just stared at him.

"I'm surprised you haven't noticed any symptoms, any discomfort, something that would have brought you to a doctor some time ago."

"I don't know what I should have noticed."

"Frequent urination at night, lower back pain."

"I thought I was just getting older. I thought everybody had those things."

"Chills and fever, night sweats."

I was quiet. He watched me.

"You've had night sweats."

"Yes." I thought of waking, of dreams, of Jeanne drying me off, calming me.

"The bed actually gets soaked from your sweat."

"Yes."

"And no bells went off?"

I shook my head. "I always attributed it to recent events, stress, food I'd eaten, something like that."

"And stomach pains? Abdominal discomfort?"

"Yes. It would last a week or so, but it always went away. I thought I needed more fiber in my diet. Or stomach flu. Same thing. It didn't register."

The prescription sat on the desk between us. "Your reaction is a common one."

I took the paper, folded it, put it in my shirt pocket. "This is curable? I'm going to be okay?"

"It's treatable. You're going to be okay. I'll see you in six weeks. We'll go from there."

"You said I'd been sick a long time." I was standing, putting on my coat. "How long?"

"Can't tell. But I'd say it's been years."

Years. I digested the word. "How many years?"

"Can't tell. Could be up to ten years, from what I saw."

I looked at him. "I thought I was just getting old," I said.

He nodded, shrugged. "You are," he said. "But not that old." He held out his hand. "See you in six weeks. Get a sample jar from the receptionist on the way out."

I looked down, took his hand, shook it. I had new numbers to think about. Six weeks. Fourteen million. Ten years. They explained lots.

I FINISHED the coffee and sandwich, left the Food Court, left *The Collegian* on the table, left Ashland, Ohio, got back onto I-71. I wanted to get as close to Cleveland as I could before it got dark. I don't like driving at night.

II

I'VE MENTIONED regrets already. I've thought of another one. Dad wanted a new window in his room—the room he had when he lived with Jeanne and Adam and me—that he could open more easily than the one that was there. It was an old house, and most of the windows were the wooden ones with ropes and pulleys, ones that had been painted over countless times. When you lifted the clunker in his room, you battled the warping of the years, those coats of paint.

He mentioned it several times. I worked on it a bit, chiseled, sanded, but not too seriously. Finally, one day at dinner, he offered to pay the cost of putting in a new one. I agreed that it sounded like a good idea. But I was reticent to let him pay, and I couldn't afford it just then. So it kept getting put off. In the spring. Maybe next fall.

Driving on I-71, heading to Cleveland, I saw the window, propped with a wooden stick, saw the fan on his dresser circulating the air. Wished I'd paid. Wished I'd let him pay. It was too late.

"YOU NEED to do something. You need to be of use."

I'd heard my father say this many times.

"Sometimes," he'd said, "just sitting in this room, I get thinking too much. I get to brooding. You have to do something, or you brood."

He did small jobs around the house, and we encouraged them. The basement was his personal domain. He painted the oil tank a fluorescent silver, wrapped every visible water pipe with insulation, poly-filled cracks with gusto. These were jobs that his bad eyes could handle—as long as they occurred in the basement where hardly anyone saw the results. In the kitchen, it was a little trickier. Every night when I came home, I'd rewash the day's dishes. He just couldn't see enough detail to get them completely clean. And he liked to help by mopping and washing the kitchen floor. Mostly he just pushed the dirt around, and we'd find it in massed, wet piles in corners. Again, it was no big deal. It was easy enough to finish the job when he wasn't around.

One morning—I can't remember why—I came into his room when I didn't know he was there. He was propped on his bed doing sit-ups. The man was in his late eighties. I was impressed. I don't even do sit-ups.

"I don't want to die," he said to me one time.

173

I couldn't think of anything to offer in return.

"I don't want to miss anything. I want to know what happens to you, to Adam. I want to know what happens to everybody."

I WENT back to see Samuelson six weeks later. He was such a veteran he could give you an estimate merely by looking through the microscope.

"You're up around twenty million." He lifted his head from the lens. "Very good. Excellent, actually. You're responding well."

"What does this mean?"

"We're going to attack it more aggressively. I'm going to prescribe a heavier duty antibiotic. Really go after it."

I followed him to his desk in the other room, sat down.

He handed me the new prescription. "Six more weeks," he said. "Any problems before then, let me know."

I SAW Samuelson every six weeks for a year. For the final few months, he returned to the original, milder antibiotic—less expensive, fewer side effects.

My last visit, though, was memorable.

"You're a miracle," he said to me.

"Am I?"

"You're at fifty million. Tremendous progress. That's a normal sperm count. Motility's good. You've responded wonderfully."

It was everything I wanted to hear. Over the intervening months I'd heard, twenty-eight million, thirty-five, forty. "I'm cured?"

He smiled kindly. "It's never really cured. It's managed. You'll always have some white blood cells. You still get the occasional days of stomach pains, night sweats, right?"

"Yes."

"And you will. I'll give you two prescriptions for antibiotics, ten days worth each, for when it recurs. If it becomes too uncomfortable, fill one of the prescriptions. Take the sulfa pills—with plenty of water. Don't let it go untreated. But we're going to take you off this daily regimen. You can't stay on antibiotics forever. And I can't see any reason why you can't go home and make a baby."

I wanted to phone Jeanne right then and there.

He smiled, rose from his chair. "C'mere," he said. "I'll let you see something."

I followed him back into the other room.

"Over here." He was standing by the microscope. The glass slide was still beneath the lens. "Have a look."

I stared at him, at the microscope.

"Go ahead." He stood back.

So I looked. I bent forward, focused. Slowly, inadvertently, my mouth opened.

I could hear Samuelson chuckle.

"Jesus," I said. I could see sperm swimming wildly in every direction, brimming with energy, tails wriggling furiously. In this one drop of semen, life was teeming.

I couldn't take my eyes away. It was a door into another universe. Inside me, every minute of the day, with my every breath, life was percolating, boiling, fifty million of these were searching for an egg to penetrate, to fulfill a blind destiny, salmon leaping at a waterfall.

Finally, I straightened, wet my lips, looked at Samuelson. "What do you think?"

"Incredible," I said. "Unbelievable."

He nodded, smiling. "I've been doing this every day for years," he said. "I never get used to it."

I watched him take off his eyeglasses, wipe the lenses with a tissue.

"And you're right," he said. He shrugged. "It's incredible."

III

I STAYED on I-71 all the way into Cleveland, watching for a place to stay for the night. Before I knew it, though, I was caught in the flow of traffic, swept along into the urban center, missing the less-expensive motor hotels and inns on the city's outskirts. Then I got lost, ended up traveling west along the lake's edge. It was dark when I pulled over on a side street and unfolded my map, holding it close to the windshield to catch the light from a streetlamp.

I turned around, went east, back the way I had come, followed the bright lights, the tall buildings, ended up on Lakeside Avenue, turned capriciously when I saw a familiar name, Ontario Street, crossed another street whose name was duplicated from city to city—St. Clair Avenue—and saw the Marriott. I stopped.

It wasn't what I had in mind. But I was tired, disoriented, and ready to stop driving.

YOU CAN rationalize anything.

I told myself that I deserved a little luxury, a nice hotel, a treat, after a Best Western, a Hampton Inn. When I finally got into my ninth-floor room, though, which turned out to be half the size of the former two, at twice the price, I gave up my rationalizing. I had to admit it. It was actually a step down. Another big city had taken a bite out of me before I'd mustered any defense.

IN JAKE'S, the bar downstairs, I ordered a Bud, opened a couple of the city maps available at the Information desk, tried to figure out where I was. I had to eat dinner.

The Flats, a developing area on both sides of the Cuyahoga River that twisted through Cleveland, was nearby. It seemed promising. It said that *Cahagaga* was Mohawk for "crooked river." I liked it. Sounded touristy.

What the hell. The hotel hadn't quite worked out. Maybe dinner would. Back in my room, I made a reservation at a restaurant called Watermark, profiled in "The Critics' Choice of Cleveland's Best Restaurants," showered, changed my clothes. I got the Honda out of its underground parking, made my way onto Old River Road in the Flats, let myself be seated at a table by the window overlooking the brown Cuyahoga River.

It wasn't Pizza Hut. It wasn't Chi-Chi's. I had a nice salad with Romaine, mesclun, iceberg lettuce, and croutons, tossed with carrot, scallion, and Romano cheese; the dressing was a honey rosemary vinaigrette. For an entrée, I ordered Lake Erie walleye—coated in a blend of mustard and cracker crumbs, served golden brown, with Ohio grown broccoflower and carrots. Just to make sure I hadn't forgotten my roots, though, I ordered a Guinness, always a complement to seafood.

Over coffee, I watched the late July sun set over the river. Nice. Very nice.

Jeanne, I thought. Adam.

I missed my family.

—◆—

BACK AT the hotel, I rode the elevator up to my compressed Marriott cubicle. Sitting on the bed, I phoned home, told her I'd be home tomorrow evening. Told her to expect me.

STILLWATER, MAD River, Crooked River.

I dreamed I got separated from companions at a bazaar, surrounded by tables with mounds of exotic foods. Wandering among brightly colored canvas, along dirt footpaths, I examined bowls of spices, desserts of nuts and syrup cut into small squares, until I was confronted by a Gothic building—elaborate stonework, ivy—set against a river. I went inside, looked into vaulted rooms with leaded windows, great fireplaces, high ceilings, finally descending worn stone steps out the back way, opened a domed wooden door, and walked down to the water. It was twilight. The evening crackled softly, perfectly: streaks of dark clouds in a pewter sky. The river was still, a wide ribbon, a sinuous mirror. I watched sleek birds plummet from above, tucking their wings flush to their bodies, projectiles, diving beneath the surface, emerging with fish, lifting off once more into the air, circling, high.

A woman approached, dressed in a long gown, asked me to take her picture against the slate and purple sky.

At the water's edge, bending down, I picked up a small, round, smooth stone, closed my hand on it. I looked about me, at the dream, knew it was real. Knew everything was real. I squeezed it tightly.

In the morning, I awoke feeling rich, lucky, comforted. Beside the bed, on the night table, was the stone. The new one.

Sixteen

I

Music needs a shape. Sydney has the Opera House, a concrete jester's cap with vaulted roofs angling away like the blossoming of a Fourth of July explosion, dominating the city's harbour. Cleveland has the Rock and Roll Hall of Fame, hundreds of glass windows tapering up, slanting back, pyramiding to a point, among towering white concrete disks, points, jags, a sentinel on Lake Erie.

The sun reflected hotly off the cement of the expansive circle that skirted the entrance where I stood. It looked like, I thought suddenly, the landing target for a spaceship that might descend from above.

It was 10 A.M., Saturday, July 29, 1995. The information in the pamphlet in my hand told me that groundbreaking had occurred on June 7, 1993. Billy Joel, Pete Townshend, Sam Phillips, Sam Moore, Dave Pinter, along with the inimitable Chuck Berry, had witnessed the event. It would open to the public on Saturday, September 2. I was five weeks too early.

I looked at it, the angles, the lines, the curves, and I could see the music. When I closed my eyes, I could hear it. I could hear the crying. I had learned something from Bobby Swiss.

Back on Monday the twenty-fourth, when I'd left home, I'd told Jeanne I'd be gone three days, maybe four. It had been six days now. I took one last look, listened one last time, got into the car, rested my arm out the window, saw the broad, imposing hood of my long-gone 1960 Chev through the windshield, got onto I-90, and headed for Toronto.

THERE'D BEEN one other trip—a big one. After my year of antibiotics, with renewed hope, Jeanne and I planned another vacation getaway. In July, two years ago, a month after Chuck Berry had watched the earth being turned out where I had just stood, we went to Ireland for a week. I'd never been. I'd listened to hand-me-down stories all my life. And I had to admit—the idea of a trip back to some roots held great romantic appeal. After 150 years, I'd be the first in my family to return.

We flew first class, paid the extra bucks for it—champagne, cheeses, smoked salmon, and hot, moist towels handed to us with silver tongs to wipe our hands and faces. Almost embarrassing. Almost. The other thing I remember about the flight over is the little girl in the seat ahead of us being afraid, watching her father comfort her, envying him.

IN DUBLIN, we stayed at the Gresham on O'Connell Street, a four-star hotel picked from a guidebook acquired from the Irish Tourist Board back in Toronto. It was nice, but overpriced—in the same way as the Marriott in Cleveland.

After the obligatory catch-up day due to flight exhaustion and time difference, the next day of sightseeing and fish and chips and pubs and a fine Indian dinner at Saagar on Harcourt Road, we got into the swing of it. We had an Irish breakfast of eggs, sausages, bacon, black pudding, and beans, bought a handwoven-in-Sligo woolen blanket on Grafton Street, checked out of the hotel, rented a standard-shift Nissan Micra, and, literally, headed for the hills. We'd come across the ocean for romance, to make love. To make a baby. It wasn't going to happen in the Gresham. We didn't want it to happen in the Gresham. It was out there somewhere, under wild Irish skies, in the soft green mountains.

We were crazy. It was fun. It was exciting. In Rathmines, on the way south out of Dublin, we stopped at Quinnsworth Supermarket and bought fresh bread, salmon, cheese. Flying first class had made an impression. At the Off-Licence beside it, we bought beer and wine.

GLENDALOUGH, IN the Wicklow Mountains, sounded promising. St. Kevin, in the sixth century, had chosen it as a place to become a hermit. Eventually, he founded a monastery there, and what remains today is an ancient monastic village: a series of churches, a stone tower, all in ruins, except for a small structure known as St. Kevin's Kitchen, dating from the eleventh and twelfth centuries. We'd seen pictures of a beautiful and desolate place, a glen with two lakes, the valley's sides rolling with woodland.

What we got was hundreds of tourists. Buses emptied on a regular basis, parking was nonexistent. We left our beer and wine in the car, wandered about, finally sat on a bench and ate our bread and cheese and salmon, drank mineral water that cost a pound a bottle.

A groundskeeper saw us sitting there, out of place, and spoke with us. He nodded in the direction of a group of young people. "Foreign exchange students," he said.

We looked at them, at the cameras slung over their necks.

"Like kindergarten students," he said. "That's the way they behave." Using tongs, he picked up a soiled condom from the grass at the edge of the path, shook his head, deposited it in his garbage bag, muttered something under his breath, left us there.

I knew there was someplace you could still go to be alone, to be a hermit if you wished. But it wasn't here. Not anymore. Not a Sunday afternoon in the summer at any rate. You could feel a bit of the magic, still there, just under the surface, but you couldn't get to it. St. Kevin, I thought, must be praying feverishly as he looked down.

WE STAYED in the mountains, drove west, saw a waterfall tumbling over a green hill. Near Carlow, we stopped to see a dolmen—the Brownshill Portal Tomb—dating from between 4000 and 3000 B.C. It was fenced off, with an explanatory "Office of Public Works" sign, otherwise untouched. The entrance to the burial chamber of a portal tomb is marked by two tall stones, covered with a single massive capstone that rests on them, sloping downward and to the rear. The sign said that this one weighed 150 tons and was probably the heaviest of its kind in Europe.

Unexcavated, it said. We stood amid the giant rocks, atop hidden pottery shards, stone beads, flint arrowheads, ornaments that had once been important to their bearers, atop the bones of farmers, warriors, druids—we didn't know—and gazed across the now-civilized fields, hay bundles stacked neatly.

⸺◈⸺

In Castlecomer, north of Kilkenny, we pulled in at the Avalon Inn, ivy-covered, white wrought-iron fence, roses, rented a room. We had dinner at the Lion's Den in town. I had the pork chop, Jeanne the curry chicken. Both came with chips. Afterward, back at the Inn, tucked into a snuggery in the pub, we ordered a Jameson's and a Guinness each, finally relaxed, went upstairs. We made love in the shower.

We discovered that it wasn't easy to get lunch once you got into the countryside. Finally, in Newtown, a crossroads south of Tipperary, we stopped at a neat, whitewashed building with the name O'Brien and a Guinness sign on its exterior.

"How didjas end up here?" The gentleman setting the ham sandwiches and pints in front of us had gray hair, his sleeves rolled up to his elbows.

"Our Michelin Motoring Map," I said. "Scenic routes are marked with this heavy green line." I took it from my pocket, set it on the counter, showed him.

He looked at it, studied it, nodded. "They know a thing or two," he said. "Prettiest view in Ireland is only a couple miles from here." He pointed at a spot on 664, just north of where we were. "Have a look. You can see the whole of the Glen of Aherlow. The Gaity Mountains in the background. See for miles. Take your breath away."

"You're O'Brien," I said.

"I am," he said. "Do the lady and yourself a favor." He smiled, knowingly.

We went, we parked. Green and brown fields as far as the eye could see. The clouds touched the gray-purple mountains in the distance. We tried to guess how far away they were. Ten, twenty miles? We couldn't tell. It took our breath away.

Just as things began to creep into our heads, a car drove by, slowed, pulled over. We looked at one another, shrugged. Jeanne touched my arm, said softly, "Let's go."

A COUPLE of hours later, south of Clogheen, in the Knock-mealdown Mountains, at a place called The Gap on our map, we parked again, got out, looked around. It sounds a little corny to say it, but it was stunning—so beautiful, it hurt our eyes. The slopes about us were green, brown, purple, fern- and heather-covered. In the distance was a stand of pines, a blue lake, isolated, nothing on it. In another direction, fields, fresh, flat, the horizon touching the sky. If O'Brien could see this, I thought, he might have to reassess his vistas.

I felt Jeanne beside me, close. "Whatta you think?" she asked.

I listened, looked around, eyes adjusting to the depths and distances. Silence. Solitude. It was sunny, sixtyish, white clouds dotting above.

I nodded. "I think so."

She smiled, white teeth glistening. A finger tucked a strand of hair behind an ear. For a moment, looking at her, I felt dizzy.

I slung the bag with the beer, wine, bread and cheese, the hand-woven blanket we'd purchased in Dublin, over my shoulder, and we headed up the slopes, toward the sky, away from the world. And we did what we came for.

Like the outdoor lovemaking at the cottage back on Paudash Lake in Ontario, everything was so right, so good, so perfect, the landscape became both erotic and sacred.

St. Kevin had been right. Getting away from people could be a balm. He would have liked it here, I thought. Very much. I think he would have liked it even more if he'd had a woman with him.

In the late afternoon, the sun soft, we fell asleep, half-dressed, hidden among the ferns.

II

"NOW *THIS* is a storm." I had to slow down. The Micra's windshield wipers could barely keep up with the rain, and the narrow road we were traversing—not to mention driving on the left-hand side—made me doubly cautious.

It was 3 P.M., two days later. We were on 344, in Connemara, County Galway, the brooding, wind- and rain-swept Maumturk Mountains on our right, the Twelve Bens rising on our left.

"I have to go to the bathroom." Jeanne looked sideways at me.

I had to agree. It had been a while. "Not a bad idea."

I'd been trying to drive through the storm, get far enough north, see if it abated in Mayo or Sligo. But it was getting worse, blowing in off the Atlantic. The weather reports on the car radio were calling it a gale. I'd never been in a gale before.

"There." She pointed.

My gaze followed her finger. Light yellow, two stories, eight windows across, three peaks in the roof. A stone fence, crushed gravel driveway lined with painted white stones. "Must be a hotel. Or a lodge." Here, I thought. In the middle of nowhere.

"Let's see if we can use their bathroom."

Made sense. I welcomed the chance to stop. Any excuse would do, but this one was starting to make real good sense.

We'd spent last night in a B and B in Gort (fifteen Irish pounds per person), the previous evening in the Central Hotel, Mallow, County Cork (twenty pounds each). Walking through the doors of Lough Inagh Lodge, we knew we'd moved up a notch. The lady behind the desk was charitable, understanding, listened to our exotic accents, and steered us to the washrooms—the most immaculate we'd encountered in Ireland, including the four-star Gresham back in Dublin.

Finishing before Jeanne, I idled, strolled about. I wandered into a library, tastefully appointed, an open log fireplace surrounded by wing-back chairs, poked my head into the dining room, checked out the oak-paneled bar—again, complete with fireplace.

"This place is gorgeous."

I turned and looked at Jeanne, who had appeared behind me. "Not bad, is it?"

"Why don't we see if they've got a room?"

"It's the middle of the afternoon."

"Have you looked outside? Have you forgotten?"

I hadn't forgotten. "Might be a budget breaker."

"We can ask."

She was right. We could ask.

"WE HAVE one room. A cancellation. It's sixty pounds per person."

We were quiet for a minute. We translated it into dollars, first Canadian, then American. Either way, we could feel the Irish rain, wind, and fog settle onto our backs.

"Might be more than we want to spend."

"I understand."

And she did. It was completely understandable. With resignation, we understood it too.

A half hour later, the windshield wipers beating furiously, we pulled over, got out our maps, oriented ourselves again. Visibility on all sides was a couple of dozen feet. We were here, in Connemara, God's country, but we couldn't see it. A sudden gust of rain and wind lashed at the side of the car, rocking us slightly.

Jeanne sighed. "I don't know about you," she said, "but I've got my sixty pounds right here." She pulled the notes from her purse, fanned them out. She raised one eyebrow. "Where you gonna stay?"

IT WAS a corner room on the second floor. With the rain and mist, gray clouds sliding up the mountains, the view across the lake was haunting. And the room itself—a canopy bed, sitting room, dressing room adjacent to the bathroom—it was everything one might expect for one's sixty pounds.

Jeanne wore her black dress to dinner: white wine, smoked salmon appetizer, leek and chive soup, prawns in garlic butter, white chocolate mousse dessert with kiwi coulis. We took our tea in the library, then retired to the dark-paneled bar, seated ourselves in front of the fireplace, pretended we could afford it all.

The bartender, in his early twenties, placed the Baileys in front of me and the Irish Mist on Jeanne's coaster.

"Any chance we could get you to put a peat fire on for us?" I nodded at the ornate, black iron hearth.

"No problem." He smiled. "We call it a turf fire."

"Oops."

"Have you one going in a minute."

WE WERE the only ones in the room. Jeanne put her feet up on a wooden stool, settled back, let the warmth penetrate as the bartender stood back, ran a hand through dark, black, curly hair, watched the turf logs do their work.

"There," he said.

"It's great." Jeanne was glowing. "Thanks again."

"My pleasure."

"You from around here?" she asked.

"I'm from Galway. I rent a place nearby."

"Is this a summer job or full-time?"

"It's summer for me this year. But I hope to learn some of the business this way."

"You go to school in Galway?"

"No, Limerick. University of Limerick."

"I have a son about your age," she said. "Just started university last year. In Toronto."

I thought of Adam, his summer job, working at Mr. Lube on Overlea Boulevard, in the pit, staring up at the bottoms of automobiles while we sat here, tucked away from reality.

He looked surprised. "Excuse me for saying so, ma'am, but I wouldn't have picked your accent as Canadian."

"And you'd be right. I'm Kentucky." She nodded at me. "He's the Canadian."

"She is too," I said. "She just doesn't know it yet. What are you studying?"

"I'm taking a business degree. Specializing in what they call Leisure Industry—recreation, tourism, hotel management, like that. I can learn here. It's Ireland's fastest growing industry. I'd be involved with places like this, folks like yourselves. I think I'd enjoy it."

"You're a smart young man. Smarter than I was at your age."

He smiled. "I try to tell my girlfriend the same thing. She's home in Galway. I see her as often as I can."

I tried to orient myself. "How far is that?"

"Forty-six miles. But who's counting? It's easier for her to get up here than it is for me to get down there, what with my hours, working weekends and all."

"You got your own place near here?"

"No." He shook his head, smiled. "Can't afford it. I have a room with a family in Recess, few miles down the road."

Jeanne was eyeing him. "What's your name?"

"Brendan."

"What's your girl's name?"

"Darla."

"What do you and Darla do when she comes up for a visit?"

I met her eyes, wondered at the question. "Why, they play checkers, Jeanne. What else?"

He laughed, didn't answer.

But Jeanne persisted. I realized she was fishing. "You must have a place you get away to, away from here, from the lodge, just the two of you."

I began to see where she was heading, admired her anew, leaned forward, interested in what his answer might be.

"There are some nice places," he admitted.

"Suppose my husband and I wanted to get away by

ourselves, off in the mountains. You know," she was openly coy now, "a picnic, alone. Where would you suggest?"

"Assuming it stops raining," I added.

"Ahh," he said. "You can head out in just about any direction hereabouts and be alone."

"Your special place," she said. "We won't tell." Her voice lowered. "In fact, we won't even be here next week, won't even be in the country. Your secret's safe with us."

He hesitated, studied us, looked down, smiled, looked up. He shrugged. "There's one place." A pause. "Very private. Very pretty. Only the locals know it." He leaned a hand on a table, relaxed. *Tobar agus leaba Pádraic. Mám Éan.*"

We listened to the Irish, to the old language, its lilt flowing from him suddenly like a brook.

"St. Patrick's Well and Bed. Pass of the Birds. It's a holy well." He could see that we weren't sure what he was telling us. "Do you know what a holy well is?"

I felt a small embarrassment. "Not really. I can guess that it's a place of worship, a special place."

"There are probably thousands of them all over Ireland." He scratched his head, thought for a moment. "They're sacred places, ancient places. People make pilgrimages to them, seeking something. Say prayers, what have you. Most of them aren't very accessible. Not the kind of thing most tourists are interested in—too hard to get to. It's the locals who know where they are."

"Ancient places." I repeated his phrase. "How ancient?"

"Nobody knows. Pre-Christian though. The Celts? The Druids? Then they got all mixed up with Christian beliefs. They say that St. Patrick climbed to the top of the *mám*, looked down on Connemara, gave it his blessing."

He smiled. "Lots of folks dismiss it as childish superstition, but I think they miss the point."

Jeanne and I were quiet. With the smell of the turf fire, here, far from our everyday world, we were listening to a twenty-something student bartender. It was we who should be telling him things that he did not know. We were the world travelers, old enough to be his parents, surviving quite comfortably in a city of three million. But we were both smart enough to know what we knew and what we didn't know, and to shut up when in the presence of the latter.

"People have psychological needs, you know. Anyone who has gone on a pilgrimage—taken a special trip for anything—knows what a pleasurable and memorable experience it is." He shrugged. "We're all looking for something. Something to ease the spirit, to give us hope. Something that interests us profoundly."

"You're a smart young man, Brendan." Jeanne looked at me as she spoke, then back at him. "Darla's a lucky girl."

"If I get a job, she's a lucky girl. That's what her father would say. I can hear him now."

"What do people pray for at the wells?" Jeanne asked.

"Depends. There are different kinds of wells. Seashore wells, mountaintop, bog wells, and mountain pass wells like *Mám Éan*. Some pray for sick children, some for various ailments—backache, headache, you name it. They say that many people used to pray for children of their own, to have them, that the wells were symbols of fertility." He smiled. "Last thing most people want now, right?"

We didn't answer. I don't know about Jeanne, but I suddenly felt like I was outside, alone on a hilltop, the gale winds buffeting me.

III

WE WERE lucky—the weather cleared the next day. Although last night's dinner wasn't included in the sixty pounds each, breakfast was, so we helped ourselves to poached eggs with salmon, black pudding, orange juice, potato cakes, and sliced tomato, then sat back and finished our tea before checking out.

"IF YOU go south," Brendan had told us, "back down 344 the way you came, about half a mile, you'll come to a single-lane road running off to the left, into the mountains. There's a sign in Irish there: '*MÁM ÉAN, Tobar agus leaba Pádraic.*' *Tobar agus leaba*—Well and Bed. Go about two miles along it. It's narrow, but you can drive it. A few hundred feet before you come to where it takes a ninety-degree turn to the right, there's a place to pull over. You can't miss it. There's another sign posted there. In Irish." He smiled. "You'll have to go on foot from there. Follow the track up to the top of the pass—about another half mile." He thought again. "Maybe a mile—I'm not sure. It's at the top." He looked carefully at both of us, hesitated, added: "There's an old children's burial ground on your right as you start up the path. Off a few hundred feet. No markers like you might be thinking of. Just stones, piled in special arrangements. Hundreds of years old, they say. You can tell it's man-made, not a natural part of the landscape."

WE SAW the old children's burial ground on the way up. A stone ring, fifty feet diameter, stones arranged within, part of a small stone wall still standing. We passed by in silence.

We were in a world of stone. At the summit, the *mám*, there was an array of artifacts—almost a small monastic site. Our eyes hurt as they adjusted to the startling depths and distances. We stared at the Twelve Bens that rose up, touched the clouds, ten, fifteen, twenty miles away. Beside us, a statue of Patrick, mounted atop a loose rock base, gazed with us across the mountains and the glens and the rivulets and the loughs. Fourteen Celtic crosses, each mounted atop a pile of loosely pyramided stones, were spread over the pass: the Stations of the Cross, the fourteen scenes from the Passion of Christ on his way to Calvary. The inscriptions on each were in Irish.

Behind Patrick, a stone oratory had been built into the mountainside, a small, open structure, with an arched roof and an altar, where a Mass could be said. I stared down the mountainside, pictured the crowds that had gathered over the centuries.

Our man Brendan could teach *Bord Fáilte Éirann*—the Irish Tourist Board—a thing or two. He was in the right business—it was a natural calling. He'd told us that among the pre-Christian Celts the year was divided into four quarters: spring, February 1, was the feast of Imbolc; summer began with Beltaine, May 1; autumn was heralded by Lughnasa, August 1; and winter with Samhain, November 1. This well, usually visited on the last Sunday in July, was a Lughnasa festival site.

We were ten days early. There was no festival, no crowd, nobody. We were alone.

"TELL US about what people do who'd like a child," Jeanne had said.

Brendan became quiet, looked at us with new eyes. His voice softened. "It's quite likely that people prayed for children, like they prayed for everything else, at many holy wells, but would never speak of it."

She persisted. "Besides praying, what do they do when they go there?"

I was quiet. Brendan was quiet.

"They must do something."

"There are lots of old stories. A woman can bring an egg-shaped stone as an offering. I've heard it said that she should deposit the stone in the well and then walk around it once. There's a stone bed there too."

"A what?" I asked.

"*Tobar agus leaba Pádraic. Tobar* means 'well,' *leaba* is 'bed,' *agus* means 'and.' Patrick's Well and Bed." He paused, thinking. Then: "There are different kinds of these stone beds around Ireland. Some are long stone rectangles, kind of containers, slightly concave, long enough, wide enough, to hold a person. The one on *Mám Éan* is a bit different. It's a small cave, a natural formation, almost like it was carved out of a cliff on the west side of the pass—across from the well and slightly above it. Some folk climb into it, lie there, probably say a prayer. Or whatever." He smiled. "I've done it."

"And Darla?" Jeanne asked.

"She's done it too." He was still smiling.

IT WAS a poor man's Stonehenge. But the same care, the same sense of the sacred, of the power of place, hovered everywhere. There were two stone circles, several standing stones, and a miniature pyramid. The interiors of all of the circles were filled with small stones.

"THERE'S A dark lake, very small, some thousand feet or so down the *cnoc*—the hillside—to the south. *Lough Mám*

Éan. You'll be able to see it. They say there's a salmon and an eel live there," Brendan said, "and if you see them, you'll have your wish granted. It's another good story." He leaned back, one elbow on the polished bar. "The well itself—some drink from its water, some fill bottles and take it with them. Maybe they drink it. Maybe they rub it on an afflicted area. Maybe they just save it. I don't know." He shrugged, remembering. "My grandmother says the earth is sacred. Water is the source of life. It's simple, she says. Water is a good thing." He looked at us. "I've got a flask of it. So does Darla." Another shrug. "What's the harm?"

THE WELL was girded by rocks piled in a U-shape, the approach to it littered by thousands of small stones. The water was crystal clear, no more than ten inches deep. Votive offerings were scattered about—coins, rosaries, buttons, ribbons, rusted crucifixes—anything to mark a visit.

Jeanne took the oval stone from her pocket, dropped it in the well, walked once around it. She dipped her plastic water bottle beneath its surface, held it there, let it fill. In each of the stone circles, we deposited another of the single round stones that we had brought with us, adding to the pile that had settled into the earth, century after century.

Singly, we climbed into the shelter that was St. Patrick's Bed, lay there for a while in silence. Then, when the sun squeezed through the clouds, lighting the entire pass, we climbed down, left the haven, and headed down the hillside to the small mountain pool that was *Lough Mám Éan*. By its edge, we spread out the Sligo blanket, lay down, touched, made love. Later, we sat, squinted into the distance, at purple slopes, at shaded glens, and when I turned to look back into the waters of the lough, I thought

I saw, just for a moment, a single moment, but I couldn't be sure, a flash of silver beneath its dark surface. I held my breath, looked again, but it was gone.

On the way back down the mountain, we passed the children's burial ground, again in silence.

TWO DAYS later, flying over Greenland, heading home, the pilot announced that it was minus forty-three degrees Celsius outside the aircraft. We looked down at the blinding white, at the mountains that no one would ever touch, and I thought once more of the silver flash in the water. I thought of the salmon and the eel.

IV

UNDERSTANDING, FOR me, seldom comes quickly. I have no way of knowing if it's like this for others. I was crossing the border into Canada at the Lewiston bridge, just north of Niagara Falls, when things finally fell into place—tumblers finally meshing, after years of tinkering, jimmying. Probably it was the memory of *Mám Éan*, the proximity of the Falls, I don't know, but I saw the pattern: Las Vegas, the drive-ins, Niagara Falls, the Poconos, the cottage on Paudash Lake, the Rock and Roll Hall of Fame—even Dayton and the Legacy Lounge, Mamma DiSalvo's Restaurant, all the colleges and universities growing like grain throughout Ohio. They were all holy wells. The sacred was the secular, a pilgrimage was a pilgrimage. We visited places in hope of change, peace, nourishment, insight, understanding. If we were lucky, very lucky, we fed our senses—ate, drank, experienced love, erotic or otherwise—at the same time. Listened for the music.

I touched my shirt pocket, didn't breathe. The stones. Both of them, real, still there. It was getting dark. Traffic was light. I figured about two more hours to home. Jeanne. Adam.

I tried not to drive too fast.

Seventeen

I

IT MUST have been the late 1980s. At dinner one night, Dad told us how he'd heard on the radio that every household was going to get a Blue Box, provided by the city, into which you'd put all your used jars, bottles, cans. This was to be set out with the garbage, to be picked up for recycling.

"You mean we're supposed to separate our garbage?" I was skeptical.

"That's what they said. Said we'd have to clean out the cans and bottles too."

"What? That's ridiculous. Wash our garbage. It'll never happen. What are they thinking?"

He shrugged.

"People won't do it. They're dreaming. It'll never work."

"That's what they said." He shrugged again. "Doesn't seem so bad to me. Should work."

I shook my head in disagreement. Jeanne and Adam remained quiet.

"The window in my room is sticking again."

"I'll see what I can do. After dinner."

There are conversations that stick in your head. I think

of this conversation every time I see a Blue Box, every time I wash out an empty can of tomato paste, a mustard jar. How stupid I was.

"WHAT WAS the stupidest thing you ever did?" I asked him another time.

"Too many to choose from."

"Off the top of your head."

He swiveled in his chair—the one that's still there, the green one, in the back room. "I had a banjo, a beautiful one. It was a Gibson—manufactured in Kalamazoo, Michigan. I'd bought it in Detroit. Mother-of-pearl inlay, nickel-plated. Paid five hundred dollars for it—back in the twenties. Can you imagine? I was in Detroit, playing a job. The Sioux City Seven. That was what we called ourselves." He paused. "It's a long story." A half smile. "I got drunk. I got into a cab and left it on the curb. Didn't even notice until I got to the hotel. Told the police. Spent an extra day in Detroit." He looked at me. "Sixty years ago. Never got it back." The shrug. "It's still out there, somewhere. I wonder about it lots, who's got it."

"Jesus."

"Off the top of my head," he said. "If I were to go farther down into this old skull, I'd sink in stupidity like quicksand."

"Maybe I shouldn't have asked."

"Nah. Doesn't matter, not now. It's what you don't have, what you lost somehow, that's what sticks, though."

I could hear the front door opening, Adam coming home.

"It's out there somewhere," he said. "Just think. Mother-of-pearl."

—*∿∿*—

AFTER THE Ireland trip, with still nothing happening by the fall, we began to wonder again. The ball went back to Jeanne. Siliaris referred her to an obstetrician-gynecologist who specialized in fertility problems.

He told her that they'd exhausted every preliminary investigative route, that the only thing remaining was exploratory surgery to find out what was going on inside.

"Like what?" She told me she'd asked.

"Ovarian cancer. Blocked fallopian tubes. Endometriosis. We don't know," he'd said. "Laparoscopic surgery. A simple procedure. Done in the morning, home by evening. Do you experience strong pain during menstruation?"

"I don't know what strong pain is. I don't know what I'm supposed to feel. But yes, I get pain. What's endometriosis?"

"A chronic condition. Nobody's sure what causes it. Cells from the uterus lining also grow elsewhere in the pelvic area. Can cause pain, cysts, even blockages. Probably the leading cause of infertility."

"I DON'T know what to say." And I didn't. "It's up to you."

"It seems so radical."

"What's this laparoscopy?"

"Minimally invasive surgery. Instead of cutting a big hole that needs weeks to heal, they use special instruments that fit through a few tiny punctures. One of them is called a laparoscope. It's a special video camera. They watch what they're doing on TV. Must be like that movie—*Fantastic Voyage*."

"It's still surgery. They still have to put you out."

"It ain't a day at the beach."

JEANNE THOUGHT about it over the winter. In April, she booked herself in, had it done. She was home by dinner.

They found one of her tubes blocked and endometriosis. They said they'd cleaned up most of the latter while they were in there, but that it could recur. Her other fallopian tube was still ovulating normally. You only need one, they'd told her. You'll ovulate every other month.

Sometimes we do stupid things. Sometimes stupid things just happen to us. I had had night sweats. Jeanne had had severe cramping. But we were patching ourselves up, mending what had broken over the years, giving ourselves a chance. Everyone needs another chance. It could still happen.

AT MISSISSAUGA Road, I pulled off the QEW and stopped for a coffee and donut at a Tim Hortons. I phoned home. She answered. I told her I'd be there in about half an hour. Told her I was back.

I wanted to get home, park the 1960 Chev, put it away.

II

IT WAS midnight. We sat at the round, plastic table on the back deck in the humid July night, the air still and heavy, a single candle between us, unmoved by any wind, condensation forming on chilled glasses of white wine.

There are many ways to make love. When I had gotten home, ours had been frantic, with the freight of absence and a deep longing. Now, calmed, wearing T-shirts and shorts, we stared at the night shapes of maple trees, the lights from neighboring houses, the permanent glow of the city. We were alone. Adam was wherever twenty-one-year-olds went on Saturday nights.

Cool fingers touched my arm. I closed my eyes, sat there, thought of the woman by the river in my dream, her flowing gown, the birds diving toward the water, heard her ask me to take her picture.

I opened my eyes. Jeanne smiled, a smile so happy my heart ached.

WHEN I heard the front door open, I rolled over in bed and glanced at the bedside clock: 2:10 A.M. Adam. I wanted to talk to him, shake his hand, just touch him, see his face. Jeanne slept soundly beside me.

I sat up, slid quietly out of bed, got my robe, and opening and closing the bedroom door behind me, went downstairs.

I expected to see him in the hall, but he wasn't there. I wandered through the dining room, into the living room, stood there, listened.

"Leo."

I turned. He was in the kitchen. But it wasn't Adam. It was my father, Tommy Nolan, in his early forties, about the age he was when I was born. He was sitting at the kitchen table, in the place he always sat.

"Your mother has had a baby. You've got a brother."

I didn't say anything.

Steam trailed from the coffee mug in front of him, mixed with smoke from the cigarette sitting in a tin Walkerville Ale ashtray—one we always left on the bookcase in the living room. He lifted the mug to his lips, drank, set it back down. "She wants to call him Dennis. What do you think?"

I realized that this must be another of my dreams, held my breath, felt my heart pounding.

"I like it," he said. "Good, strong name. Dennis Matthew. Matthew was my father's name, and his father's too. It's my middle name."

I moved slowly into the room, suddenly dizzy, pulled out a chair, sat opposite him, folded my hands on the table in front of me. His sleeves were rolled up to the elbow, the way he liked. I could see every detail, the hair on his forearms, the threads in the buttons of his shirt, the slight slant of wire-rimmed spectacles. I was afraid to speak. He might disappear.

"It'll be our last. Your mother's thirty-nine. I'm too old now too." He smiled, lifted the cigarette, drew on the smoke.

The red garnet ring, his electric razor, the lamp in the middle bedroom, the two round stones on the dresser upstairs. I didn't know what I thought, didn't know if I should speak. But when I finally managed words, what came out surprised even me. There, in the kitchen, I asked my father, suddenly: "Do you believe in miracles?" And as soon as I'd asked it, I regretted it, afraid he would vanish, afraid that whatever was holding him here would dissolve, that the moment, this perfect moment, would fade.

But he stayed. Nothing changed. His fingers touched the coffee mug, then lifted the cigarette from the ashtray. He answered me. "Life is a miracle," he said. "Death is a miracle."

The table under my hands was real, solid. I could see

the lights of the city through the back windows. I surprised myself again with what I wanted him to know, what I had to say, now that he was back, for however brief a time. "Jeanne and I are trying to have a baby." The moment froze, crystallized, melted. I felt the runoff, warm, then cold, then gone.

He met my eyes, stared at me. "I know," he said.

I saw him in front of me, felt him in front of me, a presence, the air electric.

"There's a line drawn across your life." Smoke trailed from the cigarette in his fingers. "When you become a parent, you cross the line forever. It's the dividing point. You can look back, but you don't want to go back. You go forward. You're glad to go forward. It is the only thing that makes sense."

Again, afraid he would go, afraid he would leave me, I tried to seize the moment. "I don't know what to do. I don't know what I want. I don't know what I'm looking for."

He nodded. "You give your children away. You give them to the world, then the world happens to them."

In my head, I heard the coffee table in the motel split in half, explode as it touched a world I could see only now.

"Life will happen to you. You'll try to shape it, but it will happen to you." A pause. "What do you think you're looking for?"

My head swam. "You," I said, looking at him. It seemed true. Then, feeling my chest constrict, almost breathless, words came out that I didn't know were there, truer words. Softly: "My son."

The cigarette tip brightened. He took it from his lips, held it over the ashtray. The smoke curled up toward the kitchen ceiling, a slow spiral. "Maybe your son and I are the same."

I stared at him, knew the moment couldn't last, knew it was almost over, knew that was why it was like a diamond, perfect. He ground the cigarette out, sipped the coffee one more time, and I wondered if it was instant coffee, his standard before he lived with us. Then he pushed the chair back and stood up, stood opposite me. "You don't understand, Leo. You've crossed the line already." He looked down into the empty chair beside him, then placed a hand on the shoulder of a young man in his twenties, strong, tall, who had not been there a second ago.

A heartbeat. Another. I closed my eyes, opened them. I put my hand to my chest, felt faint, thought momentarily that this must be what it feels like to die, thought I must have died, as I understood, finally, what I was seeing. He was the age that he would have been if he had lived.

Side by side, one standing, the other seated: grandfather and grandson. Tommy Nolan took a stone from his pocket, a perfect, round stone, placed it in Aidan's hand, pressed the young man's fingers closed on it. "Ron gave this to me," he said to him. "One of my sons. You should have it."

I watched, could say nothing. A dream, I thought. A dream that had become a vision, then a prayer. A prayer that would become a dream again, cycling, forever.

Then Aidan looked at me, smiled, the stone clutched tightly, and spoke to me, at last, after all these years, words that fell like soft rain. His eyes crinkled, blue, bright, pinned me. "I'm okay, Dad," he said. "Don't worry."

My head rang. Elbows on the table, I leaned forward,

put my forehead in my hands, squeezed my eyes shut, squeezed till I saw exploding suns. I don't know if I cried or not. I can't remember.

When I opened my eyes, they were gone.

I WAS still sitting there at two-thirty, when Adam came in the door.

"You're back." He was wearing a white T-shirt, jeans, sneakers.

I looked up at him, smiled. "I'm back." A shrug. "Couldn't sleep."

"Mom asleep?"

"Yes."

"How are Uncle George, Aunt Amanda? Everything okay?"

Cincinnati. I'd forgotten. "They're fine. Everything worked out."

"Great. Jane and I were at a party. Just got her home." He was at the sink, filling the kettle. "You want a cup of tea? Help you relax. Might put you out."

I shook my head. "No. Thanks."

"I'm gonna have one. Gonna read till my eyes close. Sunday's my day off." He flashed a smile over his shoulder. "Ain't it grand?"

I had to agree. "It is." I stood up, went over to him, squeezed his shoulder, thought about everything, realized there was nothing I could say, not yet, not now. "See you in the morning."

"Make it the afternoon." He plugged the kettle in, turned to me. "Mom missed you. She didn't say it, but I could tell."

I looked at his face, his strength, his youth. "I missed her. I missed you both."

He grinned.

"Good night." I chucked him on the arm, touching him one more time.

"Night."

The kettle began to whistle as I headed up the stairs.

IV

St. Patrick's Bed

I can understand myself only in the light of inner happenings. It is these that make up the singularity of my life.

—CARL JUNG

Memories, Dreams, Reflections

Eighteen

I

IN THE morning, both the ashtray and coffee mug were still there. They were empty, though. No butts, ashes, no coffee stains. Clean as a whistle.

But I could smell it. So could Jeanne.

"Somebody's been smoking," she said. She looked at the ashtray, then at me, strangely. "Not you."

"Not me."

"Can't be Adam."

"I don't think so."

"You're not telling me."

"I don't know what to tell you."

She hesitated. Then: "Tell me everything's okay."

I reached out, twisted a finger in the hair, touched her neck. "Everything's okay."

She came close, tilted her head against my chest, closed her eyes, breathed evenly.

My hand went to the back of her head, her hair soft in my palm.

"WHATCHA DOIN'?" I asked, standing at the bedroom door.

Adam, seated in front of his computer console, smiled. "Surfing."

"Surfing," I repeated. I liked saying it. It made me feel young. "For what?"

"That's the beauty of it. You go in any direction. Bob and weave. Links here, there. You never know where you'll end up. Follow a whim."

"For instance."

"For instance, I typed in '1990 Toyota Tercel.' My car. The windshield wipers are seizing up. Wanted to get some information or advice, what to do."

"And?"

"Found out there's a linkage that's probably jammed. I'll see what I can do without taking it to a garage. The rad's pretty shot too. Jesus, you should see it. Found some prices on a new one."

"How much?"

"Two-fifty. Three hundred."

"You got the money?"

"You kidding?"

"We'll work something out." I shifted my weight, straightened in the doorway. "I thought you said there was a random flow to your surfing. Sounds pretty focused to me."

"Remember Madagascar?"

"Mm?"

"Fourth largest island in the world? My anthropology class?"

I remembered discovering that he was actually taking anthropology. "It's coming back to me."

"Look." He clicked on something. A menu popped up. He highlighted a line in blue, clicked again. A photograph of strangely shaped trees against a red sky crept slowly down the screen, text overlaying it. "Baobabs. Upside-down trees."

Another click. The image changed. People carrying what looked like a shrouded body through a village square.

"What am I looking at now?"

"It's right in the middle of death dancing season," he said.

I was quiet.

"June to September—winter down there. Malagasy families unearth loved ones from their tombs, dance with them, then carefully rewrap them for reburial before the warm weather."

I walked over to where Adam sat, stood behind him, stared at the screen.

"It happens every five years. They update their ancestors on family gossip too. Then they wrap them in new cloth, put them back, inside the family tombs, with something they liked in life—a favorite drink, food. They attend to their needs."

A coffee mug. An ashtray.

"It's not morbid. It's joyous, celebratory. They call it *famadihana*."

An electric razor.

Adam shrugged. "Just surfing. It's interesting. Whatta ya think?"

"What's it mean?"

"What?"

"That word. *Famadihana*."

"Literal translation is 'turning of bones.' Everybody gathers round, toasts them with beer, Coke, sings songs, wears party hats. Wild, eh?"

The red garnet ring. The tackle box.

"And it's not just in remote communities. Right outside the capital too. Organized by businessmen, professionals, academics." He turned, looked at me. "You think it's nonsense? Craziness?"

I thought of the holy well and bed at *Mám Eán*, heard Brendan's words. *Lots of folks dismiss it as childish superstition, but I think they miss the point.* "No," I said. I had both hands on his shoulders now. "I think maybe they're onto something."

I missed my father. I missed my mother. I missed everybody. I saw Aidan's hand closing over the stone, squeezing. "I think I know what you should do," I said.

"About what?"

His shoulders in my hands. "About going to see your father. Later this summer."

He looked up at me. I thought of Donny Swiss, his half brother, marking maps in the pocket guide to Dayton with a yellow highlighter.

"Go," I said. "See him." See them both. Hear the music. "It's the right thing to do."

We stared at one another. His eyes widened.

I nodded. "I'll help you."

II

TWO WEEKS later, Adam and I took his Toyota to Uptown Motors on Queen Street and had them drop in a new rad. With tax, it came to $299. I put it on my Visa. Next day, we drove up to Mr. Lube on Thorncliffe Drive—where Adam had worked the previous summer—to get a checkup and oil change. They replaced the air filter, PCV valve, wiper blades, told him everything else was okay. Before I could offer, Adam paid for it himself, with cash.

"How much?" I asked on the way home.

"They gave me a discount. As an old employee, you know." He grinned. He never did tell me how much.

Through the windshield, I looked at the new wiper blades. "You get that linkage problem straightened out?"

"Last night. After dinner. Fixed it myself."

I stared at the five o'clock shadow, his hands on the wheel, smiled.

ON MONDAY, August 28, 1995, Adam left for Dayton with Bobby Swiss's address and phone number folded into the back pocket of his jeans. Jeanne and I watched him drive down the street, the August morning lightening in the east. He hit the horn once, quickly and lightly, a wave out the window, then was gone, around the corner.

Twenty-one, I thought. When anything is possible.

I looked at Jeanne. "It's early. Why don't we treat ourselves to breakfast?"

"Where?"

"McDonald's?" I got the smile from her, the one I wanted, the one that tells me how lucky we both are.

"Big shot. You always know how to treat a woman." Her eyes held me: a touch of Kentucky rain, soft. "You still think he'll be okay?"

I looked at her. "He'll be fine." The street was empty, the air beginning to warm. "If there's a kid out there with his head screwed on better than his, I'd like to meet him."

She was quiet. Then: "Thanks."

"For what?"

"Everything."

"The McDonald's breakfast?"

"Yeah. Right. The McDonald's breakfast."

Then the smile reappeared, a summer's end smile, melting me.

III

WE DIDN'T hear from Adam all week. Then, after dinner, Friday, September 1, five days later, he came through the front door. He was home.

JEANNE LIT the outdoor candles and we sat on the back deck. I remembered she and I alone here, a few weeks earlier. I remembered she and I sipping warm beer from long-necked bottles of Bud, on the veranda of her place in Ashland, Adam with a Coke, a summer evening, eleven years ago. The past and the present, together.

Adam took a swig of cold Sleeman's ale, put it down on the plastic table, let the ring of condensation form at its base. "Good," he said, sighed. "It was a long drive."

I filled two glasses with what was left from the bottle of white chardonnay in the fridge, placed one in front of Jeanne, sat down with mine. "Cheers."

We clinked bottle and glasses.

Waited.

Adam looked down, thinking.

Without tension, the moment stretched. It would happen, I knew. Words needed to be chosen. You can tell too much. Adam knew it too.

"I took your advice, Leo. Stayed on the outskirts, at a Days Inn." He touched the beer bottle, made a line in the droplets. "Phoned him Tuesday, told him who I was, said I was in town, asked if I could see him."

He paused, but not for any dramatic effect. It was an honest pause. We could see that the words were coming slow, not doing justice to memory, feelings.

"He seemed pretty surprised at first. Then he was quiet for a minute." He shook his head. "Jesus, we were both quiet. I was almost dizzy."

I was almost dizzy listening. I glanced at Jeanne, saw her jaw rigid.

"He asked me to hold the line while he talked to his wife, then came back and said that she thought I should come to dinner the next night, what did I think of that? I asked him if he'd like that, and he said, yes, he thought he would, if I would." Adam shrugged. "So I went. The next night."

"WE HAD meat loaf. He asked me if I'd like a beer with dinner. I said whatever he was having, so he opened two." Another pause, thinking. "I met his wife, Pam. And I met his son, Donny."

I watched Jeanne's face, but couldn't read it.

"I have a brother." And then he smiled. And when he smiled, Jeanne relaxed, and I saw the edge, the touch of relief, the start of something close to wonder, close to happiness, and found myself smiling too.

"HE HAS a life." He was talking to his mother now. "He works at Delco. His wife takes care of Donny, who is sixteen, but has a medical problem and needs her." When he didn't elaborate, didn't dwell on it, my admiration for him stirred. "We had a nice evening." Then he nodded, remembering. "Very nice." He reached in his pocket. "He gave me this."

I stared at the audio cassette he placed on the table between us: *Roy Orbison—In Dreams: The Greatest Hits*.

"I listened to it in the car on the way back. Good stuff. He knows a lot about music."

Looking around me now, at the two of them, at the city, the August night, I could hear the music.

"Will you see him again?" It was the first thing Jeanne had asked. I watched Adam lock eyes with his mother.

He was quiet for a moment, then shrugged. "Maybe."

We listened. Waited.

"It's not as important now." He was still staring at his mother. "But I'll keep in touch with Donny. I'm going to write, phone. I'll see him again. Somehow." Then he turned to me, spoke to me. "He told me I didn't need him. Said I had a good father already."

Our eyes met.

"Said to say hello to you, Leo. And that Donny loved his guide to Dayton."

Jeanne looked at me.

"He also wanted me to tell you that you owed him a buck for a pool game. And that Mamma DiSalvo says you're a good tipper."

Jeanne and Adam were both still staring at me when I closed my eyes. That was when I heard him say it to her.

"He said, tell your mother that I'm sorry."

When I opened my eyes, Jeanne's cheeks were wet. But she was smiling. She was smiling. And so was Adam.

"ONLY THE Lonely," "In Dreams," "Running Scared," "It's Over," "Crying." Adam put the tape on in the living room and we left the screen door open so we could hear it on the back deck. We finished our drinks, talked. We listened to

Roy, to that unearthly voice, heard him hit those high notes, way up there.

IV

IT WAS the second weekend in October, the beginnings of oranges and yellows, when I finally stood back, placed the paintbrush in the tray, admired it, proud of myself. I'd knocked out the old one, measured, framed it, bought the replacement at Home Depot, screwed it into place, caulked the seams, and had just finished the final coat of paint.

The air outside had cooled. Everything would change, then return again, the seasons rolling round. The past, the present, the future.

See, I said to him. You got your new window. Slides open like a dream, anytime you want. Wide open. Look out there. Feel that breeze.

He smiled. I know he did. He didn't want much. He never had.

And that night, lying in bed, eyes open in the dark, Jeanne beside me as always, Adam just down the hall, the walls of his room lined with new cracks, always new cracks, I thought of Brendan and Darla, on a mountain in the west of Ireland, beneath wild skies, taking turns lying in St. Patrick's Bed. I thought of Uncle Jim, of Nanny's parents, dealing with the cards life had dealt them, adopting children, of Phil Berney, Jeanne's father, with a baby in a laundry basket at his feet. Then I closed my eyes and looked through the microscope again, saw the life that was teeming, coursing through my body, through all our bodies, swimming upstream against all odds, thought of the plastic bottle of water on the shelf at the back of our bedroom closet, of a silver flash beneath dark waters of a mountain lough. It could still happen, I thought. Yes. It could happen.

About the Author

Terence M. Green was born in Toronto, Ontario, Canada, in 1947. He is the author of seven books, among them the novels *Shadow of Ashland* and *A Witness to Life,* both of which explore the same family that is at the heart of *St. Patrick's Bed.* A five-time finalist for the Aurora Award (Canada) and a two-time World Fantasy Award finalist, Mr. Green is a graduate of both the University of Toronto (B.A., B.Ed) and University College, Dublin (M.A.). Married with three sons, he lives in Toronto. For more information, you are invited to visit the author's Web site at www.tmgreen.com.